THE STUTTGART
NANNY MAFIA

BOOKS BY
SUSAN FLETCHER

Dragon's Milk
The Stuttgart Nanny Mafia

THE STUTTGART NANNY MAFIA

SUSAN FLETCHER

A JEAN KARL BOOK

ATHENEUM 1991 NEW YORK

Maxwell Macmillan Canada   Toronto
Maxwell Macmillan International
New York   Oxford   Singapore   Sydney

Atheneum
Macmillan Publishing Company
866 Third Avenue
New York, NY 10022

Maxwell Macmillan Canada, Inc.
1200 Eglinton Avenue East
Suite 200
Don Mills, Ontario M3C 3N1
Macmillan Publishing Company is part of the Maxwell Communication
Group of Companies.

First edition
Printed in the United States of America
1 2 3 4 5 6 7 8 9 10
Designed by Kimberly M. Hauck

Library of Congress Cataloging-in-Publication Data

Fletcher, Susan, 1951–
The Stuttgart nanny mafia / Susan Fletcher.
p.   cm.
"A Jean Karl book."
Summary: In an effort to gain more time alone with her mother, Aurora schemes to
get rid of Tanja, a nineteen-year-old au pair from Germany.
ISBN 0-689-31709-3
[1. Au pairs—Fiction. 2. Mothers and daughters—Fiction]
I. Title.
PZ7.F6356St   1991
[Fic]—dc20

90–23225

FOR KELLY

CONTENTS

THE STUTTGART
NANNY MAFIA

NO ANSWER

I'm sitting here in my bedroom with the door locked and I'm never coming out.

Well, not for three days, anyway. Not till Wednesday, when we all have to go to the airport. I'm staying right here in my room, and nobody can make me leave.

I've got some peanut M&M's stashed in my desk drawer so I won't starve to death. And if Patsy would ever answer her phone, I could get her to come over and smuggle me some cookies. Maybe even chocolate chip. Maybe when she hears I'm starving in my room for three whole days, she'll bake a giant batch of cookies for my Time of Trouble.

Mrs. Sandberg had a Time of Trouble last winter when she slipped on her front steps and threw out her back. The whole neighborhood came rushing over to her house with cookies and cakes and pies and stuff. Even my mother baked a pie, which would have been a miracle except she found a recipe for pie with no sugar and no crust and only

1

oat bran sprinkled on the top. Mrs. Sandberg gained twenty pounds. From the other stuff—not the oat bran.

I dial Patsy's number again.

Ring.

Ring.

Ring.

Come *on*, Patsy.

Ring.

No answer.

I slam down the phone.

The tricky part is going to the bathroom. I don't think I really have to yet, but every time I think about it I sort of do. I wish I had my old bedroom back, because there's a bathroom connected to the bedroom and I wouldn't have to walk down the hall where someone might see me. Except I don't really want it back because it's Tanja's room now, and if it were mine it would mean that I'd kicked her out, and even if everything else that happened hadn't happened, I probably *still* couldn't face her then.

That's the thing. I can't face her. After that whole awful time up there on the mountain, at 2:00 in the morning in the snow and the dark . . . I had it all figured out—it was my most brilliant plan—but it was the stupidest thing I ever did. And when somebody looks at you like that, the way Tanja looked at me up there, and then afterward, when the real trouble comes—well, how can you ever face that person again?

No answer to that one. So I'm staying right here in my room.

Maybe I could face her if I only knew for absolute certain that she wouldn't say something nice. If I had a three-day, money-back guarantee that she'd ignore me or stick out her tongue or say something snotty, then I'd come right out. I could handle that.

But, knowing Tanja, she would say something nice. In spite of the blizzard and the brownies and the spy notebook and the slugs. In spite of what's going to happen . . . I wouldn't even put it past her to *forgive* me, or something horrible like that.

I couldn't take it. Every time I *think* about that, my face goes all trembly and my nose gets all tingly and my eyes start tearing up. . . .

Stop it!

I'll think of something else.

Chocolate chip cookies.

Gigantic cinnamon rolls.

Pizza with pepperoni and double cheese.

Brownies with frosting—no nuts.

Tanja.

I wish I'd never met her.

No, that's a lie.

I wish I *could* wish I'd never met her. Or that I could start all over again. Like reversing the tape on a VCR but making a whole new movie on it. I'd start when Tanja first came . . . no, before that, when Mom and Benjamin first told me about Tanja . . . no, after that, when I was explaining to Patsy. . . .

Patsy.

Patsy, where are you?
I dial again.
Ring.
Ring.
Ring.
No answer.

I'M GOING
TO HATE HER

The whole nanny thing was Benjamin's idea.

"Aurora," he asked me, way back in September, before I'd ever heard of Tanja or Stuttgart or people who say *w* when they ought to say *v*, "how would you like to have a nanny?"

"A nanny?" I crunched down on the last of my oat flakes. "You mean like Mary Poppins?" I could just see her blowing across Blue Heron Lake, clutching that beat-up umbrella of hers.

"Well, no, Aurora, not exactly," Benjamin said, stirring honey into his tea. "Mary Poppins isn't a real person."

"I *know* that," I said. "I was joking."

"Oh. Of course." Benjamin chuckled sort of nervously and glanced across the table at my mom, who was scraping Stewie's breakfast off his face, hands, and hair. Benjamin glances at Mom a lot. After two years of being my stepdad, he still doesn't have the hang of me. Mom says it's because

5

he wasn't around kids very much before we came along. Sometimes I wonder if he was ever a kid, himself.

"Actually, she would be an au pair girl," Mom was saying now, "which is different from a nanny." She set Stewie down on the floor and gave his diapered rear a pat.

"A what?" I asked. "Oh pear?"

"Au *pair* is French for 'on a par with,' meaning she would be just like a member of our family."

"Like a big sister," Benjamin put in.

"Let me get this straight," I said. "You're buying me a big sister from France?"

Mom sighed and began swabbing the glop off of Stewie's high chair. "Here's the thing, Aurora. Benjamin and I have been thinking. . . ."

Uh oh. I felt the old familiar clutching-in-the-stomach that came whenever Benjamin and Mom got to thinking. It meant something was going to change. Something I liked the way it already was.

Benjamin-and-Mom thinking was what turned Mom into a health food fanatic. One day she was a perfectly normal mom, baking cookies and pies and stuff. The next day everything had oat bran in it.

Benjamin-and-Mom thinking was what ended Mom's and my Wednesday night bowling. We'd been doing it for five years, ever since I was six. Then the two of them signed up for dancing lessons Wednesday nights—that was the only night for beginners, Benjamin said—and bowling just sort of got dropped.

The very first time Benjamin and Mom got to thinking,

they wound up getting married, which is when *everything* started to go wrong.

I hate it when they think.

". . . thinking about my going back to work."

"*What?*"

"My hygienist is leaving," Benjamin said. "Dr. Morton said your mother's the best dental hygienist he's ever had."

"Wait a minute," I said slowly, not quite understanding, not *wanting* to understand. "Mom? You're going to work with *him*, instead of staying home with Stewie and me?"

"Your mother needs to get out of the house. She misses her work. Don't you, Shelley?"

Mom wrung out the sponge and turned to look at me. I could tell from her eyes she felt guilty. "Look, Aurora," she said. "We're just going to try this for a while. And we'll have a German au pair girl come live with us to take care of you and Stewie."

"German?" My mind wasn't working so well. It felt numb. "I thought you said French."

"Her name is Tanja. She's nineteen years old and she lives in Stuttgart, Germany. We got a letter from her yesterday. She seems very nice." Mom rummaged through a drawer. "There were some pictures. . . ." She pulled out a handful of photos and handed them to me.

I flipped through the pictures, not really looking, mostly just waiting for my brain to kick in. Mom was going to work with Benjamin. She wouldn't be home in the afternoons to listen to me tell about my day or to go out for frozen yogurt. She'd be with *him* all the time—hardly with me at all. This . . . this blond person in the pictures was coming to stay with us. To live with us.

Then I thought of something else. Where? Where would she stay?

"She's staying in the guest room, right?" I asked.

This time they both glanced at each other. "Well, we were thinking about that too," Mom said. "She would really need a larger space—"

"To entertain her friends," Benjamin finished. "She would need a bathroom connected to her bedroom, so she wouldn't have to—"

"*My* room?" A hot little jet of anger spurted up inside me. "You're giving her *my room?*"

"Well, that will be up to you, Aurora," Mom said. "I want you to think about it, though, and do what you think is—"

Crash!

Shriek!

Stewie sprawled out on the floor, clutching a depotted philodendron. Dirt from the upended flowerpot spilled across Stewie and the rug.

"Oh, Stewie!" Mom ran to clean up the mess. I followed.

"You've already decided all this, haven't you?" I said. "You're going away from me all day long so you can be with him. You're kicking me out of my room. You've got this whole big plan, and it's going to mess up my life, and you never said a word to me until it was too late. You never even *asked* me. I can't believe it!"

8

"You're not the only one in this family," Benjamin said. "You were an only child too long, Aurora, and it's time you learned—"

"We didn't want to tell you until we knew for sure," Mom said, looking up from brushing the dirt off Stewie. "Listen, I'll make a point of spending special time with you—I promise. Just the two of us."

"Like you did with bowling?"

"We'll start bowling again. Soon. I don't know how I let that lapse."

"That's the beauty of this arrangement," Benjamin said. "*Tanja* could take you bowling any time you want." He glanced at Mom, then added quickly, "Or your mother, too, of course. The point is you can go bowling more often now. And I think you're really going to like Tanja once you get to know her."

"Like her?" I spun around and stumbled past Benjamin and out of the room. He didn't understand—not a bit. I stopped for a moment, then stuck my head back through the doorway.

"I'm not going to like her," I informed them all. "I'm going to *hate* her."

BEFORE BENJAMIN

Before Benjamin, things were different.

Back then, Mom did all her thinking with me. I guess she used to think with my dad, too, before they got divorced, but that was a real long time ago. Now Dad lives in Malibu, California, with his new wife, Lydia. When I was little, I used to visit them for practically the whole summer, but I haven't done that in three years. Not since they had their baby.

When it was just the two of us—Mom and me—she worked for a dentist, Dr. Morton. But when she came home, she was all mine. Sometimes she read me stories, or let me fix her hair. Sometimes I thought up ideas, and we did them together. We made forts out of blankets and tables and chairs. We wrote messages in invisible ink. We invented fun dinners. Orange dinner was carrot sticks and orange slices and macaroni and cheese. Round dinner was meatballs and brussels sprouts and baby potatoes. Nibble dinner was peanuts and peas and canned corn.

I know that sounds babyish. But it was neat.

We never have fun dinners anymore.

Saturday mornings, when it was Mom-and-me, we'd go down to the Laundromat and, while we were folding the clothes, we'd think of different plans for the afternoon. Then we'd vote on our ideas.

I got to use two hands.

There was a special thing we did on Christmas Eve. First, Mom made a fire in the fireplace, and lit our three fat red candles. Next, we turned off all the lights in the house. Even the Christmas tree lights. Then, when the room was all warm and rosy and flickery, we told each other stories. Christmas stories. We had to make them up—that was the rule. I remember leaning against her, and letting my eyelids droop, and following the thread of her stories through the dark. Her stories were always longer than mine.

And after that we opened all our presents—except the Santa ones.

And after that, we roasted marshmallows. That was my idea.

Nobody I know has ever heard of roasting marshmallows in the fireplace on Christmas Eve. When I tell them, some people say it's dumb.

But it wasn't dumb. It was . . . I don't know . . . *ours*. It was our own special thing, that we did on Christmas Eve.

Only now we don't do it anymore—because of Benjamin.

WE DON'T NEED YOU, MARY POPPINS

*F*irst thing I did after they told me about the nanny was call Patsy.

"You mean like Mary Poppins?" she asked.

"Of course not like Mary Poppins. Mary Poppins isn't even a real person."

"I know that, Aurora. But I thought, you know, maybe the nanny'll take you and Stewie out to fun places and stuff. I bet she likes to sing and dance."

"I don't care what she likes to do. We don't need Mary Poppins or anyone like her. I'm old enough to take care of myself, and Mom can take care of Stewie. She's been doing it ever since he was born."

"Supercalifragilisticexpialidocious," Patsy sang.

"Would you cut that out? This is serious! I don't need some dumb, foreign, substitute mom coming in and telling me what to do."

"Did you say foreign? Maybe she'll be Austrian, like in

The Sound of Music, where Julie Andrews is a nun, only she doesn't want to be and—"

"Patsy!"

"The hills are aliiiive," Patsy sang.

"Patsy, would you get serious? We're not talking about movies here. We are talking about my *life*. We are talking about some blond, German, nineteen year old that Benjamin is bringing over here to boss Stewie and me around while Mom goes to work with him. He *says* he needs a hygienist, but I don't believe him."

"Are you sure, Aurora? Maybe he really does."

"There are a thousand hygienists out there all dying for that job. He wants my *mom*. He wants her all to himself. Remember I told you about bowling? What happened to that?"

"Only a million times."

"*Dancing*. At their age. And now every time the radio's on they go mooning around the kitchen, doing the *cha-cha-cha*. It's disgusting!"

"I think it's kind of cute."

"How can you even *say* that?"

Patsy just didn't get it, and I couldn't explain. My whole life felt—I don't know—like an earthquake zone or something, where the ground jerks around under your feet and after it's done, nothing's where it's supposed to be anymore and you have to grope around to find a good place to stand. And there's nothing you can do about it, and it could happen any time, and you don't even get a warning. But I couldn't tell Patsy that. It sounded too dumb.

13

Then I remembered about my room.

"But guess what, Patsy. Guess where she's going to stay?"

"Who, your mom?"

"No! This Tanja person. She's staying in my room. I'm getting kicked out. They want me to move into the guest room."

"Oh, wow. That really *is* bad."

"It's bad all right." I swallowed, feeling a lump rise in my throat.

"Isn't there anything you can do? Couldn't you refuse to move out?"

"It wouldn't do any good. She'd come anyway, and they'd figure out some way to get me to move. They've already made up their minds."

"At least you've got to try. You're good at plans, Aurora. Like that pet show you organized last summer. There must be something you can do."

"Well, I don't know. Maybe there's something. But I sure don't know what it is."

WOLF MAN

Nothing worked.

I tried pleading ("Please please *please* don't make me have a nanny") but they told me to stop whining. I tried bribery ("I'll make all the beds and I'll vacuum the living room . . . and the dining room . . . the whole house?") but they said how could I do that if I can't manage to keep my own room straight. I tried guilt ("Well, I guess I'll have to tell Mrs. Wagner that you can't help out at school anymore, like all the *other* mothers") but my mom only promised to start bowling with me every Thursday night, which she'd already promised anyway.

I even thought of a plan where Mrs. Sandberg next door would watch Stewie until noon, then she'd drop him off at day-care on the way to her volunteer job, and then Mom would pick him up at 3:30 and be there when I got home from school. Benjamin could get a spare hygienist for an hour and a half a day.

"Too complicated," Mom said.

"It's already settled," Benjamin said.

So in the end I wound up in the van on the way to the airport to pick up Tanja on Halloween day.

Halloween. When witches come. How perfect is that?

"I hope she likes her room," Mom said, squinting at the road.

"You mean *my* room," I said.

"Oh, honey, I know she'll appreciate your giving up your room. But the quilt. I don't know. What if she hates yellow? I tried to get the blue, but it was out of stock and they told me . . ."

I pulled my wolf man mask down over my head. The rubbery smell of it filled my nose. When I ran my fingers through its shaggy fur, it made a crackly, rumbling noise in my ears. I could hardly hear Mom's voice when I did that—just the high, excited tone of it and a few floating pieces of talk: "Can't *wait* to meet her," and "after all those letters," and, "can you say 'Tanja,' Stewie?"

"Ta," came Stewie's voice from where he was strapped in his car seat behind me.

I shifted the mask so that the eyeholes didn't quite line up with my eyes. I could still see out, could see the highway whizzing by, but in the van mirror I had no eyes at all—only skin where my eyes ought to be.

There was a thump on the back of my seat; Stewie let out a wail.

I twisted around in my seat and saw that he'd dropped

his bear-bear. "Just a minute, I'll get him," I said. Stewie wailed louder. Stewie shrieked.

"Aurora, take off that mask right now," Mom said. "You're scaring the daylights out of Stewie."

"I was only trying to help," I said. I peeled the mask up over my head. "See, it's me, Ror." I undid my seat belt and, leaning between the two front seats, let him touch my cheeks with his slobbery hands.

Stewie's face uncrumpled and stretched into a smile. "Ror," he said.

I considered letting him touch my mask but decided against it. For sure he'd stuff it in his mouth and drool all over it. Fifteen month olds do that a lot. I had just hauled up bear-bear from the floor beneath Stewie's seat when Mom started up again.

". . . and she'll take you to the zoo, Stewie, and she'll give you mush-you-husky rides around the house, and—"

"I *invented* that game," I said. "*She* can't play that."

"I thought you were tired of it."

I was—sort of—but that didn't mean I wanted someone else taking over.

"Listen, Aurora. You'll be free to play with your friends after school. You can take piano lessons, dance lessons—whatever you want. You—"

"If you didn't go back to work, I could do that stuff."

Mom sighed. "Aurora, we've been all over this before. Benjamin and I think. . . ."

Benjamin-and-I think. I was so sick of hearing what Benjamin-and-I think.

I closed my eyes, flooded with a sudden, sharp aching for the old days, when it was Aurora-and-I. Then, sneaking a peek at Mom, I pulled the mask back over my head. I ran my fingers across its smooth, rubber fangs, across its dry, crepey skin. I felt the way it wrinkled and pooched out in places where my own skin didn't. It didn't smile when I smiled. It wouldn't cry if I cried. I'm invisible, I thought. Here, inside the warm, moist, rubber-smelling mask, no one could see.

". . . think of her as a sister," Mom was saying. "As a new big sister whom we'll all love very much." She turned and flashed me a brilliant smile.

Inside the mask, I didn't smile back. "Great," I muttered.

"What?"

"Nothing." I shrank down in my seat.

I've got a new father and a new little brother and we moved to a brand new house. I've got the same old mother, but she's starting a new job. And she expects me to jump for joy because I'm getting a new big sister.

Great. Just great.

At the airport parking lot Mom made me take off the mask. But I slipped it inside my jacket while she unbuckled Stewie from his car seat. No thief was getting his mitts on *this* mask. It was the expensive kind, the kind that covers

18

your whole head. I'd had to do a lot of convincing to get Mom to buy it.

"Mrs. Stephanus said she'd meet us at the gate," Mom said. She picked up Stewie and set off fast through the parking lot, then down the escalator into the terminal. Stewie kicked and screamed to be let down. He learned to walk at nine months, and now he's a walking *demon*. I followed them, threading through groups of people, my arms folded against my chest to keep the mask from slipping.

Mom stopped to check a monitor. "Plane's on time."

Good. Then we wouldn't be home late. Patsy and Jessica and I were going out for pizza tonight with Patsy's family and then trick-or-treating afterward.

At the gate, Mrs. Stephanus rushed over and began talking to Mom. Mrs. Stephanus is the lady from the au pair organization who set up the whole thing with Tanja. She ruffled Stewie's hair, then peered down over her glasses at me. "Aren't you excited?" she asked.

I shrugged. Two wrinkles deepened in between Mrs. Stephanus's eyebrows; she glanced at Mom. People sure were doing a lot of glancing lately.

Now the passengers started coming in. I searched the faces for the one in the pictures I'd seen. Wispy blond hair. Blue eyes. A little gap between her two front teeth.

Mom gasped. Mrs. Stephanus was already working her way through the crowd. She stopped and began talking to someone; all I could make out was a fluff of blond hair.

19

Then Mom, clutching Stewie's hand, rushed forward. She stopped, started to shake hands, and then she was hugging the blond girl. Stewie stretched up his arms and said, "Ta," and they let him in the hug too. Mrs. Stephanus fiddled with a camera, smiling like crazy.

Something sank inside me. There was no room in that hug for me, even if I had wanted to join.

Which I don't, I thought fiercely. I definitely don't.

I hugged myself and felt something shift inside my jacket. The mask. I took it out, looked at it, then pulled it over my head. I heard my name—"Where's Aurora?" someone asked—and Mrs. Stephanus moved aside. And there was Tanja, beautiful, wispy-blond Tanja, staring straight at me with the stunned look of a bird that's flown smack into glass.

"Yah!" I said.

Tanja jumped and let out a peep. The camera flashed. Tanja's carryon slipped off her shoulder, spilling postcards and yarn and underwear. Everyone began talking at once, Mrs. Stephanus comforting Tanja, Stewie blubbering, Mom apologizing to Tanja one minute and yelling at me the next.

"Take that thing off, Aurora! Take it off now!" she kept saying, but she was so busy picking up Tanja's things that she hardly even looked in my direction.

I backed away. "It was only a joke," I mumbled, but nobody paid attention. They were all crowded around Tanja, repacking her carryon, talking to her, leading her away. I stood there watching them go, breathing the rubbery-stale air in the mask.

"What's the big deal?" I said, my voice sounding small and muffled. "It was only a joke."

MONSTER
WITHOUT A MASK

Somewhere between the ladies' room and the baggage pick up place, the wolf man mask got lost.

"I bet you left it on the sink," Mom said later. She drew the last whisker on Stewie's face and straightened his bunny ears. "I remember you took it off in the rest room. Then, when Stewie crawled into that other lady's stall and you had to drag him out—"

"I *looked* there," I said. I had looked everywhere, racing through the airport, checking all the places I'd been plus a lot of places I hadn't. But the mask had disappeared.

"I really *liked* that mask. How can I be a monster when I don't even have a mask?" All I had was a dumb old brown shirt and a pair of brown pants. I wouldn't look like *anything*.

Mom spun Stewie around and started pinning on his tail. "You're the one with all the creative ideas, Aurora.

22

Why don't you paint your face with watercolors? Then you could mousse out your hair like a monster."

"Dumb," I muttered. "I'm gonna look dumb."

I heard Mom sigh as she stuffed Stewie's chubby fists into a pair of white mittens. "Just give it a try, Aurora. It's not the end of the world." She gave Stewie's tail a final fluff, then got up and headed for the kitchen.

I followed. "I can't believe Patsy and Jessica left without me," I said. "How could they *do* that to me?"

"We were late, sweetheart, looking for that mask. And the traffic on the freeway—I can't believe it was backed up all the way to the Blue Heron exit."

"But now I have to go with all those dumb little kids and their dumb nannies—"

"Au pairs, Aurora. And keep it down."

"It's humiliating! I feel like a baby! Why can't I go by myself?"

"I've already told you, it's not safe."

"Then couldn't *you* go with me?"

"That might hurt Tanja's feelings. She's determined to go with Elsa tonight, although if I were as tired as she is, I'd go straight to bed. Come on, Aurora. It's your chance to get to know her. She—"

There was a knock at the door.

"They're here," she said. "If you're going to do something with your face, you'd better do it fast."

"Tell them to wait! I can't go like this." I fled upstairs, nearly colliding with Tanja in the hall. I pawed through a drawer for my paint box, then crossed to the bathroom.

Downstairs, I heard a chorus of "trick or treat," then a babble of voices in a foreign language. German, probably. I tiptoed into the hall and peeked over the railing. Tanja was hugging a girl with long, white-blond hair. They were squealing and giggling like crazy. That must be Elsa. Tanja had known her in Stuttgart; she was a year or two older than Tanja and she was au pairing twin boys a few streets away. Another girl, taller, with darker blond hair, stood nearby. Gudrun. I'd heard of her too. She was also from Stuttgart, but apparently Tanja hadn't known her there. Underfoot I spotted two shrimp-sized pirates, a mini-ballerina and, of course, Stewie.

Now the au pairs were speaking English to Mom and Benjamin. They all talked like Tanja, with a sort of singsong rhythm that rose at the ends of sentences as if their thoughts took shape as questions. "So happy to meet you?" "I have been here for three months?" "I do enjoy America very much?"

"Aurora!" Mom called, catching sight of me. "Come on down!"

I ducked into the bathroom. "I'm not ready!"

I wet the paintbrush and painted a V on my forehead, like the hairline on the wolf man mask. It just sort of floated there as if it had no connection with anything. Fur, I thought. Wolf men have fur on their faces. I dipped the brush in the brown again and painted little scattery lines all over my cheeks, then peered into the mirror, checking out what I'd done. It looked like some horrible skin disease. I

24

wet my fingers and rubbed the lines to blend them together like fur. Now it looked like a peeling suntan.

Fangs. Maybe fangs would help. There was no white paint in the box, so I had to use yellow. But the fangs somehow wound up not looking like fangs at all—more like a skimpy yellow mustache.

"Aurora!"

"In a minute!"

I tore down the hall into Mom's and Benjamin's bathroom and found the can of mousse. The white foam pillowed on my head, making fizzy, popping noises. It smelled like coconuts. I smeared in the mousse with my fingers, pulling my hair straight out from my head. But the mousse didn't hold. My hair collapsed around my ears, looking stringy and dirty.

I scowled my scariest scowl.

But the face in the mirror didn't look scary at all. It looked sad and kind of lost. The paint didn't hide a thing.

"This is your last chance!" Mom called. "They're leaving right now!"

"Yah!" I whispered.

CRYBABY

It was the worst Halloween of my life.

Not only because of the au pairs (who babbled away in German and flashed their cameras until tiny golden blobs floated before my eyes) and the little kids (who walked so slowly I could have hit five houses in the time they took to toddle down a single driveway). It wasn't just the disgusting fuss people made over the little kids (like, "Aren't they little *dears!*" and "Isn't this just the *cutest* ballerina you've ever seen!") and the dumb questions they kept asking me (like, "What are you supposed to be, honey?" and "Aren't you too old for trick or treat?").

That stuff was bad enough, but it wasn't the worst. The worst was yet to come.

Halfway around the block, I saw Patsy and Jessica, with Patsy's older brother, Tyler. Patsy called out, and she and Jessica came running.

"Hey, thanks a lot for waiting, you guys," I said. "Now

look who I'm stuck with." I jerked my head toward the au pairs and little kids.

"Well, you weren't home, and—" Patsy began.

"What're *you* supposed to be?" Jessica demanded. Jessica, of course, was beautiful, dressed in a sequined flapper outfit.

I started explaining about losing the mask at the airport and the traffic jam on the way home.

"You're supposed to be a *wolf man?*" Jessica asked. "You sure don't look like one."

Now Patsy was staring at the au pairs. "Hey, Aurora," she whispered. "Which one is yours?"

The au pairs were looking our way as if they expected to be introduced. Tanja started shyly forward, carrying Stewie. Slowly, I led my friends to where the au pairs stood and introduced them. I tried to pronounce the German names correctly: Tawn-ya, Ell-sa, Goo-d-roon.

"Would you care to join us?" Tanja asked Patsy and Jessica. Her *j* sounded like a *tch*, I noticed, so that when she said *join*, it came out funny, like *tchoin*.

"No way," Jessica said. "Not with *them* along." She wrinkled her nose at the little kids, then turned to me. "You can come with us."

I hesitated just a moment. Mom had said I had to go trick-or-treating with the little kids because I wasn't allowed to go alone. She hadn't said I couldn't go with my friends. Besides, I had been going to go with Patsy and Jessica in the first place. "Okay," I said.

"Wait!" Tanja said. (It sounded like *vait!*) "Just . . ."

(*tchoost* . . .) The other au pairs were talking in German to Tanja. They looked at me, then at Tanja, then back at me again. "Wait, I . . . I do not think that you should right now be going with them," Tanja said. "I did tell your mother that I will be caring for you tonight, and . . . and she does expect this." The tall au pair, Gudrun, said something else in German. "You must . . . you must do trick-or-treat with us," Tanja finished.

I stared at Tanja. I couldn't believe it. "But I was *supposed* to go with them. I was going to go with them in the first place, but we were late."

Gudrun said something in German and Tanja shook her head. "You must . . . must not," she said.

"I wouldn't take that off anyone," Jessica muttered.

"You're not my mom," I said to Tanja. "You can't tell me what to do."

"Aurora, do you think you should—" Patsy began.

"She has no right to boss me around!"

Gudrun spoke. "Tanja is responsible to do what your mother did ask her. Or else you do have trouble for you both."

"Cheez," Jessica said. "I'm glad *I* don't need a nanny."

"I *don't* need a nanny! And I won't get in trouble. I'm old enough to . . . to take care of myself." I tried to sound certain, but I wasn't real sure Mom would see it that way. I *knew* Benjamin wouldn't.

"I must . . . must tell your parents of this," Tanja said.

Go ahead, I almost said, but then I looked at her—really

looked—and something twisted inside me. Her mouth had the trembly look of someone trying hard not to cry.

Crybaby, I thought, hardening myself.

"Come on, you guys," I said. "Let's go."

Gudrun was right about the trouble.

I stayed out later than I should have, partly to show Jessica that I could and partly because of a weird little feeling that something not too pleasant was waiting for me at home.

The front door opened as I was reaching for the knob. Benjamin stood inside. "Come into the living room right now, young lady."

Uh oh.

Mom and Tanja sat together on the love seat. Mom was patting Tanja's hand, and Tanja's eyes were red.

Crybaby.

I dropped into a side chair, clutching my bag of candy.

"I'd like to hear in your own words, Aurora, exactly what happened tonight," Benjamin said.

I shrugged. "We went trick-or-treating, that's all."

No one said anything. Mom and Benjamin looked straight at me; Tanja seemed to be studying the carpet. The clock on the mantle sounded loud.

"Okay, okay, I met up with Patsy and Jessica and went trick-or-treating with them."

"All this time?" Mom asked.

"No, we went to Patsy's house for a while. Then I came straight home."

"Did Tanja say you could go with Patsy and Jessica?" Benjamin asked.

"No, I did not!" Tanja said. "I did tell her she must not go with them, and she—"

Tattletale.

I saw Mom squeeze Tanja's hand.

"Well, Aurora?" Benjamin said.

"Well, she didn't, but—"

"Did she say you *couldn't* go with them?"

"Well, yeah, but . . ." I turned to Mom. "You're my mom—not her. She can't boss me around. You said she's like a big sister."

Mom sighed. "Aurora, I know I said you could go trick-or-treating with Patsy and Jessica. But that was before we were late and they left without you. And Tanja *will* be like a big sister. But, honey, when you're with her, she's in charge. She's here to make life better for you and Stewie, but you have to cooperate. Your job is to obey Tanja. Hers is to take care of you."

"I can take care of myself! I'm eleven years old!"

Benjamin started talking about how old eleven *wasn't*, and I saw Mom give Tanja another squeeze.

Some big sister. All she does is boss me around.

The three of them—Benjamin, Mom and Tanja—faced me across the room. They were all against me. They were shutting me out. Sitting there like that, they reminded me of an old-fashioned family portrait—a portrait I wasn't in. All at once I thought of another picture, one of Mom

30

and me. She had kept it on her dresser in the old house. Her arm had been around me, and we'd both been smiling.

Mom-and-me. That's the way it used to be.

"Is that understood, Aurora?" Benjamin was asking.

I shrugged. "I guess."

"Then you're excused to go to bed."

Later—lots later—I heard footsteps in the hall. Tanja had already gone to bed; I had heard her come up the stairs and walk past to her room. *My* room.

Benjamin and Mom had kept on talking in low voices downstairs. But at last they, too, had come up. I had heard the water running in their bathroom, had heard the toilet flush. But I hadn't gone to sleep, not even then.

I couldn't, because of the dark, angry feelings that kept churning around inside me. I tried to push them out by reading a book. But as soon as my eyelids sagged the least little bit, the feelings came swirling in again.

Now the crack of light in my doorway began to widen. I shut my eyes and clenched my body into a tight ball. The footsteps paused. "Aurora?" came Mom's voice, softly.

I didn't move. The footsteps came closer, then the edge of my bed dipped. I felt Mom's hip pressing against my knees. I felt her hand gently sweeping the hair from my face.

"Love you, honey," she whispered.

I swallowed. I *almost* opened my eyes. I *almost* said, "I love you, too." But a part of me refused to unclench. I felt

Mom's lips brush my forehead, and then the edge of the bed sprang up again and the footsteps receded out the door.

I rolled onto my stomach and buried my face in my pillow. All of a sudden, my throat ached. Something inside me wanted to shake apart, but I wouldn't let it.

Tanja might do stuff like that, but not me.

I wasn't a crybaby.

BROWNIES
WITH FROSTING —
NO NUTS

For the next three days I didn't see much of Tanja. She was around some of the time, but she didn't do any au pairing. She was having "orientation."

Orientation is what an au pair gets when she first comes to stay with you. It's when your mom takes her out in the car and shows her the places she needs to know about and explains the things she'll have to do and discusses the things they need to discuss.

I bet they discussed me a lot.

Orientation is when the au pair learns how to work the washing machine and the dishwasher and the microwave. It's when she grinds the gears on the van so bad that your mom decides to give her driving lessons. It's when she gets a whole day off to go to the beach.

But at the end of orientation, the party's over. She's in charge. You can't avoid her anymore.

Tanja's orientation ended Sunday night. Monday was a

teacher workday, which meant we didn't have school, but Mom and Benjamin had to work. Which meant Stewie and I would be home all day with Tanja.

Fortunately, Patsy invited me over for the day. But I still had to eat breakfast at home. With Tanja.

How would she act when Mom and Benjamin weren't there? Was she still mad at me? Would she be mean?

Monday morning, I stayed in my bedroom as long as I could before getting dressed and tiptoeing down the stairs. I stood outside the kitchen and peeked in. There she was, feeding Stewie in his high chair. Was she mad? I couldn't tell.

Tanja looked up at me and smiled. "Aurora," she said, "and what may I prepare you for your breakfast?"

She didn't look mad. Maybe she'd forgotten about Halloween. Stewie, strapped in his high chair, waved a mushy spoon at me. I waved back. It was maybe half a minute before it hit me.

What may I prepare you for your breakfast?

"Um," I said. Mom never fixes breakfast for me, except sometimes on weekends. You're a big girl, Aurora, she always says to me. You can fix it yourself. I always pour myself cereal and milk. Sometimes I make frozen orange juice. When I'm really hungry, I fix toast too. But now here was Tanja wanting to know what *she* could fix.

"Pancakes?" I asked.

Tanja headed for the cupboard, saying something about

how her kind of pancakes might be different from my kind of pancakes and would that be all right?

"I guess so," I said. I hoped they weren't strange or foreign tasting. But how could you mess up a pancake?

Tanja didn't know where everything was so I pointed to the cupboards where Mom keeps the flour and the salt and the baking powder. Tanja's pancake wound up looking pretty much like the ones Mom sometimes makes on weekends, except this pancake covered the whole bottom of the pan.

"There you have it!" Tanja said, turning out the steaming, golden brown pancake onto a plate. "Do you have it with syrup or powdered sugar? Or maybe jam?"

"Syrup, please."

I watched Tanja walk to the cupboard to get the syrup.

"And butter."

I watched Tanja walk to the refrigerator to get the butter. It melted in golden rivers when I drew it across the pancake with my knife. I poured on the syrup and lifted a bite to my mouth.

Not bad.

"Would you like anything else?" Tanja asked.

I looked up. Anything *else?*

"Well," I said, thinking fast. "I like orange juice. . . ."

Tanja nodded and turned toward the refrigerator.

". . . and hot cocoa . . ."

Tanja stopped.

". . . and cinnamon toast."

Tanja turned to face me.

Uh oh, I thought. Here it comes.

But Tanja only said, "I do not know what is cinnamon toast."

"Just ordinary toast with some cinnamon and sugar sprinkled on the top." Actually, I wasn't all that hungry. That pancake was *huge*. But I could force myself, this once.

Stewie, I saw, was getting restless. He had already dropped his spoon onto the floor. Now he dipped his hands into the brownish gray goo and smeared it on his face. Tanja was busy opening the frozen orange juice can, so she didn't notice. She had forgotten, I saw, to stick Stewie's bowl to his high chair tray with the suction cup. He pushed his bowl back and forth across his tray. The bowl caught on the tray rim; Stewie shoved and it flipped and clattered, oatmeal side down, onto the floor.

I started to help, then caught myself and sat back down. That was Tanja's job now. "Uh oh, look what Stewie did," I said.

"Oh, Stewie!" Tanja wailed. She grabbed a bunch of paper towels and ran to clean up the mess on the floor. Stewie began to cry. "It's okay, Stewie, it's okay," Tanja said, scooping up oatmeal like crazy.

Something was wrong with the toast. The toaster made a strange, buzzing hum; black smoke drifted up toward the ceiling.

"Uh oh, the toast," I said.

Tanja squeaked and leaped up. She unplugged the toaster and jabbed the stuck toast with a fork. Stewie kept on crying; his face was turning red. I felt a twinge of guilt. I knew I ought to help. I knew how to handle Stewie better than Tanja did. But . . . *Tanja's job is to take care of you,* Mom had said.

So let her. That's what she was here for.

Tanja coaxed out the burnt toast, put in two more pieces, then bent to finish wiping the oatmeal off the floor. "In just a minute, Stewie," she kept saying. "In just a minute."

It's "just," not "tchoost," I thought, but I didn't say it. "Maybe you should clean up Stewie first and put him in his playpen," I said. "That's what Mom always does. Then he's not yelling the whole time you're cleaning the floor."

"Aurora, I do this my way," Tanja said sharply. Softening, she added, "It is only my way, I do not like that the floor is being dirty."

I shrugged. Okay for her. "Just trying to help," I said.

When Tanja was done cleaning the floor and Stewie, she set him down and got to work mixing the orange juice. She was too busy to notice when Stewie toddled toward the cupboard where the baking stuff was kept.

I didn't say anything. I *told* her to put him in his playpen. But she had to do it her way.

When at last Tanja had finished stirring the orange juice, poured it, buttered the toast, sprinkled on cinnamon and sugar, mixed the hot chocolate and heated it in the microwave, Stewie had discovered the plastic container where Mom kept the flour.

Plastic containers were Stewie's very favorite things. He considered them a challenge. The plastic container hadn't been made that Stewie couldn't break into within five minutes.

I gave this one three.

I gulped down my orange juice, stuffed the last of the toast into my mouth and softened it with a glug of hot cocoa. Tanja was putting things away and so wasn't looking at the exact moment when Stewie pried the lid off the container.

"I'm late!" I said. "Gotta go!"

Stewie tipped the container over his head. Flour billowed out in a dusty white cloud, powdering the cupboards and counters, piling in drifts upon the floor. Stewie howled; he looked like a drumstick dredged for frying.

Tanja gasped; I grabbed my jacket and zoomed out the door. Then I stopped, struck by a thought, and poked my head back in.

"In the afternoon I like brownies," I said.

"Brownies?" Tanja, standing in the demolished kitchen and brushing helplessly at Stewie, looked dazed. "I do not know what is brownie."

"In the red cookbook up there." I pointed to one of my mom's old cookbooks, from her pre–oat bran days. I started to shut the door again, then remembered something else.

"With frosting," I said. "No nuts."

JUST YOU WAIT

You mean she makes brownies for you *every day?*" Patsy asked at recess two days later.

"Sure," I said. "And you ought to see what she cooks me for breakfast."

Jessica didn't believe me. "I thought your mom was into health food," she said. "Anyway *nobody* gets brownies every day."

"Well, I do. Hey, why don't you guys come over after school today? You can have all the brownies you want."

I was feeling generous. After the Halloween disaster, I couldn't wait to see what Patsy and Jessica had to say about the service I was getting. Especially Jessica. I hadn't made my bed or picked up my clothes for two whole days, but when I got home from school my room was perfectly neat. It was like in this book I once read where this princess had a handmaiden to attend to her every whim. I planned on having a *lot* of whims.

"Are you sure your nanny will let you have friends over?" Jessica asked, coming down hard on the "let."

"Oh, sure," I said. "Au pairs are all right. You just have to know how to deal with them."

After school, we stopped off at Patsy's and Jessica's houses to ask permission, then headed for my house. A blue minivan was parked in the driveway. I felt a weird little flutter in my stomach, but I ignored it.

The moment I stepped into the house, I knew something was wrong. Tanja didn't meet me at the front door to take my schoolbag and my coat. Strange voices came in from the family room: screaming children's voices and voices talking in German. Even worse, the house didn't smell like brownies at all.

"Come on," I said, trying to act as if everything were under control.

The family room looked like a day-care center. Blankets and toys and bottles were thrown all over the place. Two identical toddler boys raced across the carpet pulling two identical rolling duckies; Stewie chugged along behind, yelling, "Guck! Guck!" A baby slept in a basket on the couch, and a little girl was scribbling in a coloring book at the kitchen counter.

"I'm home," I said.

Tanja looked up from where she sat drinking coffee with the two other Stuttgart au pairs. The coffee table was littered with photographs.

"Good," she said. It sounded like *goot*.

I waited for Tanja to get up and take my coat or offer me

brownies or ask about my friends. But she just picked up a photograph and said something in German to the other au pairs.

"Where are the brownies?" I asked.

Now all three au pairs looked up. I had the strange and uncomfortable sensation that they'd all been talking about me.

"There are no brownies today," Tanja said.

Jessica made a humming noise in her throat.

"What do you mean, no brownies?" I said. "You always make brownies."

Tanja hesitated, then said, "Today I do not." The tall au pair, the one named Gudrun, nudged Tanja. Tanja continued: "It is not my obligation to make you brownies for you every day. And they are not so good for your health."

"Ah, Aurora . . ." Jessica began.

"Just a *minute*," I said. This was not working out. It wasn't at all the way I'd planned it. I took a deep breath, then turned to Tanja. "It's your job to take care of me. My mom said so. And I want brownies."

"It is not my job to be your slave," Tanja said. "It is not my job to pick up for you your room or make for you your bed. It is good for you that you do these things for yourself."

"*You're* not supposed to decide what's good for me. You're not my mom."

"Tanja was trying to be your friend with you," Gudrun said, "but you only take advantage for her."

"Look, you weren't here when Mom said it, so you don't know. Tanja's job is to take care of me. Mom said so."

"Then maybe we should ask her?" Gudrun suggested.

I knew I was caught. Mom would never agree that it was Tanja's job to bake me brownies or make my bed or straighten my room. I'd been expecting her to find out what Tanja was doing any day and put an end to it. I thought for sure Tanja would tell her, like she told about trick-or-treating.

"I think I hear my mother calling," Jessica said. "Come on, Patsy."

"Wait!" They couldn't leave now. "We have other snacks." I hunted through the cupboard where the snacks were kept. Dried prunes, rice cakes, peanut butter . . . "Wait a minute! How about graham crackers? With margarine and jam . . ."

"*Graham crackers?*" Jessica raised her eyebrows. "Maybe some other time, Aurora. Come on, Patsy."

"Patsy, don't you go too." I was begging; I couldn't help it.

Patsy looked sorry, but she was backing away. "I don't think we came at a very good time," she said.

I stood there for a second after the front door closed. My throat ached again. The au pairs weren't talking anymore. Even the little kids were quiet. I grabbed my bag and stomped upstairs.

42

"Aurora . . . ," I heard Tanja say.

Oh, be quiet.

I flung myself on my bed, tensing against the tears.

I'll get you for this, Tanja. Just you wait.

BROKEN PROMISES

I *promise,* Mom had said. I'd heard her. *Tanja will watch Stewie on Thursday nights. So Benjamin can get his billing done, and you and I can go bowling. I promise.*

For absolute certain. Without fail.

I figured that promise had an A part and a B part. The A part was that Tanja would watch Stewie. The B part was that we'd get to go bowling.

I liked the A part almost as well as the B part. Especially after the no-brownie disaster. It made Tanja stay home because of me. The least she could do was give up one night a week. Look what I gave up for her—my room. Besides, she had humiliated me in front of my friends.

But the A part was the first to go.

It happened that very same evening, when Tanja was helping Mom do the dishes. I was multiplying fractions at the kitchen table. I figured I'd better stick close, to defend myself in case Tanja decided to tell about the brownies.

"There will be a party," Tanja said. "At the house of Elsa's boyfriend, on that mountain, Mount Hood? He will be inviting all the au pairs to come. Not only from Blue Heron, but from Portland and Beaverton and . . . all around?"

"When is this party?" Mom asked.

"Tomorrow night."

"She can't do that," I said quickly. "You promised. We're going bowling." I couldn't believe it. Tanja hadn't even been here a week and already she was trying to squeeze me out of bowling.

"Ah, Tanja, I have promised Aurora that we could go out tomorrow night."

"Yes, but it is only this one time. All the au pairs are going and I would like to meet—"

"Mom! You promised!"

"Hey, what's the problem here?" Benjamin looked up from his newspaper.

Mom explained.

"Well, Aurora, couldn't you . . ." he began. Then he looked at Mom. She was shaking her head *no*.

"Well. I suppose I could postpone the billing and stay home with Stewie. It's not as if I haven't done it before. Stewie and I are old buddies."

It's amazing to watch Benjamin shift into his Liberated Father mode. Every so often he changes one of Stewie's diapers, and then you don't hear the end of it for a month and a half. He tries to work it into every conversation.

Speaking of the world economy, when I was changing Stewie's diaper the other day. . . .

Imagine listening to that when you're sitting in a dental chair with your mouth all full of scrapers and hoses and rubber gloves. It's a wonder his patients don't gag.

"Yeah, old Stewie and I will hold down the fort," Benjamin said. "You girls go ahead."

"But Mom! You said *Tanja* was going to—"

"Never mind, Aurora. It works out the same." She stood on her tiptoes and gave Benjamin a kiss on top of his head. His bald spot turned pink. "Thanks, sweetie," Mom said.

"Yes, thank you very much," Tanja said.

"But—" I said.

"It's the same thing, Aurora," Mom said. "Stop complaining."

But it wasn't the same to me.

The next day when I got home from school, Stewie didn't look so hot.

His cheeks were all red and his forehead felt warm. Usually he won't sit in my lap more than fifteen seconds before he starts wriggling and squirming and kicking to get down. But I held him in my lap all through a "Star Trek" rerun and he hardly even moved.

Tanja took his temperature and gave him Tylenol. Mom came home early and gave him a sponge bath.

"I think he'll be all right now," Mom said. "His fever's coming down."

After dinner, Tanja left for the party. I waited around

while Mom gave Benjamin instructions on Stewie. We were about to step out the door when Benjamin called down the stairs.

"Uh, Shelley. I think you'd better come up here."

Mom stopped in the doorway. "Stewie?" she asked.

"Throwing up."

After that, everything fell apart. Mom rushed upstairs and didn't come down right away, so I went up to see what was happening. Stewie's room smelled sour. Mom was still scrubbing the carpet, and Benjamin was putting clean sheets on Stewie's crib. Stewie lay asleep in a nest of blankets on the floor. Mom said Stewie would be all right, but it didn't look as if we were going to be able to go bowling tonight. I could see that for myself.

"I'm really sorry, Aurora. We'll do it next week. *Promise.*"

I'd heard that one before.

It wasn't until later that the brainstorm came. Mom let me stay up late and watch TV, I think because she felt guilty. I was slouched way down into the couch, watching a movie about a little old watch repairman in New York City. One day this gangster with a funny accent comes into the shop and says he'll protect the old guy if he pays him $100 every month. "Protect me from who?" the watch repairman asks, but the gangster just smiles. Turns out, the money is to protect the old guy from the gangster and his hoodlum friends.

The man refuses to pay, then the hoodlums come in and

break up his shop. The man finds out that these guys belong to the Mafia, which is a gang of Italian crooks who stick together no matter what. For short, people call them the mob.

Very slowly, I began to sit up on the couch. Something was coming together, was meshing in my mind. I'd never been to New York City or known any gangsters—Italian or otherwise. But there was something familiar about this . . . this Mafia.

A bunch of guys with foreign accents who pretend they're there to protect you, but really want to take over.

This is happening to me, I thought. Only not with Italians from New York. This is a different kind of Mafia: the Stuttgart Nanny Mafia.

A rush of courage surged through me. I knew what I would do. Just like the guy in the movie, I'd think of a brilliant *plan*.

Those nannies thought they had me, but they didn't stand a chance.

I was Aurora Jane MacKenzie, and they'd better not mess with me.

PLAN A

I'm famous for my plans.

Last year at school I started a newspaper. It was called the *Blue Heron Messenger,* and all the reporters had to wear headbands with little paper wings taped on, like that Greek messenger-god who has wings growing out of his head. By Christmas, half of the fifth grade was working on my newspaper. Well, maybe a third. The principal wrote a letter to us, saying how neat it was. Then he said we had to stop writing our "50 Ways to Bug Your Teacher" column.

Another plan I had was the pet show last summer. Everybody loved it except Amy Bates, because Jason Stoddard's ferret escaped and ate her goldfish.

Sometimes my plans just sort of come to me, like the "Invent Your Own Crazy Soda Contest." Sometimes I have to brainstorm to think of something good.

This time it had to be *really* good. So I decided to get some help.

Sunday afternoon I called Patsy and Jessica, and we all went upstairs to my room for a brainstorming party. I told them about the Mafia movie and my theory about the au pairs. I taught them the rules for brainstorming. (First, you write down all the ideas you can think of—no criticism allowed. Then later you go back and decide which ones you like best.)

For amateurs, they caught on really fast.

"Spiders!" I said. "We'll put spiders in her bed!"

"Or snakes!" Patsy suggested.

"Yeah, like a boa constrictor," Jessica said.

I was sprawled out on my bed, writing like crazy. *Spiders in bed*, I wrote. *Snakes—ditto. Boa constrictor.*

"But where would we get them?" I wondered.

"Maybe somebody's got a spider collection or a snake collection the way my brother has a slug collection," Patsy said.

"You mean slugs like tokens at a video arcade or those slimy snail things without shells?" I asked.

"The snail things."

"Oh, *disgusting!*" Jessica made a face and shivered.

"There's nothing scary about slugs," I said. "She wouldn't leave because of them."

"We wouldn't have to use Tyler's slugs. He wouldn't let us, anyway. I just meant, you know, some people collect disgusting things."

I wrote *Slug collection, etc.?* in my notebook.

"Once my cousin balanced a bucket of water on top of

my door," Patsy was saying. "When I pushed it to go inside, I got totally soaked."

"Patsy, you're brilliant!" *Bucket on door*, I wrote.

"Well, *my* cousin smeared Tabasco sauce on his big sister's lips when she was asleep," Jessica put in. "Her lips burned so bad, it woke her up. She even washed off her mouth with soap, but it didn't do any good."

Tabasco sauce on lips, I wrote.

"Hey, *I* know." I kicked off my shoes and sat up so I could write better. "We could loosen the lid of the saltshaker so when she shakes it the whole thing goes on her food."

"Or get a whoopee cushion."

"Or a dribble glass."

"A rubber scorpion!"

"Fake dog doo."

"What about sneezing powder?"

"We could put bubble gum in her shoes."

"Or on the soles of her shoes."

"We could put ice cubes in her bed."

"Or peanut butter."

"We could put it on her hair."

"On her brush! Peanut butter on her brush!"

"Hold up, you guys, I can't write that fast!" My hand was cramping up, but I didn't mind. The old creative juices were really flowing. This was great! I finished writing and shook my hand to get the cramp out.

"I saw this movie once," Jessica said. "These girls

wound up their stepmother with yarn while she was asleep, then poured honey all over her. That got rid of her."

Yarn/honey, I wrote. "Hey, what about green slime! I once saw this commercial for green slime shampoo. We could dribble *that* all over her."

"We could put tape in her hair."

"Or TP her room."

"Or get that cobweb stuff they use at Halloween and string it all over her room."

"Yeah, but you can't buy that anymore," I pointed out. "All the Halloween stuff is gone."

"You're not supposed to criticize yet," Patsy said. "You're just supposed to write it down."

"Okay, okay, but it won't work." I wrote, *cobweb stuff??*

"Another thing my cousin did," Jessica said, "was light a firecracker and put it in his sister's lunch box. You should have seen the look on her face."

"That's *dangerous!*" Patsy said. "We can't—"

Jessica raised her eyebrows. "No criticism, remember?"

"Well, I still say it's too dangerous."

Firecracker in lunch box????? I wrote.

It was silent for a moment. I chewed on my pencil. Jessica inspected her nails.

"Well, let's see what we've got so far," I said. "Spiders in bed, snakes—ditto, boa constrictor, slug collection, etc.?"—

"We can't use that," Patsy said.

"No criticism!" Jessica and I said together.

52

I went on. "Tabasco sauce, bucket on door, lid off saltshaker, whoopee cushion, dribble glass, rubber scorpion, fake dog doo, bubble gum in shoes, bubble gum on soles of shoes, ice cubes in bed, peanut butter in bed, peanut butter in hair, peanut butter on brush, yarn/honey, green slime, TP room, cobweb stuff???, firecracker in lunch box?????"

"I don't know, Aurora," Patsy said.

"What?"

"I don't know if those things are going to work."

"Why not?"

"Seems like Tanja would just get mad, and you'd get in trouble."

"But if we did enough of them, she'd get the message."

"Yeah," Jessica said. "You could do *all* of them."

"I don't know," Patsy said again. "She'd get the message, but would she leave? And what about your parents? You'd probably be grounded for life. Couldn't you just tell your mother you don't like Tanja?"

"She knows that already. She'd just say I have to try harder. Tanja is Benjamin's idea, and Mom always sticks up for him, Patsy. You don't know what it's like."

I looked over the list again. Something fizzled out inside me. Patsy was right. None of our ideas seemed likely to make Tanja go home. And some of the stuff seemed . . . kind of mean. Tanja hadn't really *done* anything to me, not on purpose. . . .

I brushed the thought away. Tanja had to go, that was all.

"It's all so *obvious*, Aurora," Patsy was saying. "Everyone would know it was a trick. And everyone would know you did it. You need something. . . . I don't know. . . . something that wouldn't *seem* like a trick, at least to Tanja. Something that might really happen, like an earthquake, or Mount Saint Helens erupting—"

"Give me a break! If I could make Mount Saint Helens erupt, I would, all right?"

Jessica stretched and yawned. "Boy, I'm glad *I* don't have your problem, Aurora. When I'm in Amsterdam . . ."

There she went again, talking about Amsterdam. Jessica's father had been transferred there for a year, starting right after next Christmas. Already I'd heard more than I wanted to know about Jessica's "year abroad."

I sighed. Going up against the mob wasn't going to be as easy as I'd imagined. I read over the list again and again, trying to pull out of it the one thing that would make Tanja leave, but not get me in trouble.

It wasn't there.

I ripped the paper out of my notebook, crumpled it, and tossed it onto the floor.

It came to me in my sleep. Well, not quite in my sleep, but just as I was about to drift off. I was thinking about a video we'd seen at school about killer bees, the bees that are supposed to be coming north from South America. Every year they get closer and closer. They look just like ordinary bees, but they're more aggressive, and their stings are worse. They can't really kill you—just make going outside really unpleasant.

Then my thoughts drifted around awhile until they settled on Patsy's brother's slug collection. That Tyler! Who in their right mind would ever collect *slugs?*

Then it came to me, so hard I sat straight up in bed. What if there were a herd of . . . killer slugs? What if they were coming up from Mexico, and . . . no, then they'd have to come through California and they'd get squished on all those freeways. What if some scientist had been doing slug experiments in Oregon and had come up with this new strain, a poisonous kind of slug? And when they bit you . . . no, wait. Slugs wouldn't bite. They . . . they'd *slime* you. They'd have this poisonous slime that would burn your skin and the poison would go in so deep. . . .

Let's see, what would it do to you? Chills and fever? A permanent scar? Could you *die* from it?

I shivered. Wow. That *was* kind of creepy.

Of course, it wouldn't really have to happen. Tanja would just have to believe it *could* happen. She just had to think that Oregon was not a safe place to live.

Yeah. That was it.

All at once the old, excited feeling was back, that feeling when you've got a brilliant plan and you know it's going to work—you *know* it.

I smiled and turned over onto my side.

Plan A: killer slugs. Those critters would make *anybody* want to leave.

*   *   *

Patsy wasn't crazy about the killer slug idea. "You've got to be kidding," she said, when I explained my plan on the way to school the next morning. "Killer slugs? No one's going to believe that!"

"Why not? Everybody believes in killer bees."

"Well, I don't know, Aurora. People have read about killer bees or seen videotapes about them. Nobody's ever heard of killer slugs."

"Look, all we need to do is plant the seed of doubt in her mind. Then when she sees them . . ."

"And where are you going to get . . . uh oh. Aurora. You're not thinking of Tyler's slug collection, are you? Because he really loves those slimy old things, weird as that may sound. He's even got names for them. And besides, they aren't killer slugs, they're just ordinary old slugs Tyler found in the garden."

"I *know* they're not killer slugs! I made up that part, remember? Cheez, Patsy! I'm just saying we could make them *look* like killer slugs by leaving green slime trails on the carpet behind them. And then—"

"Green slime trails on the carpet? Boy, are you going to get it!"

"Wait, Patsy! You haven't heard the best part! I'll do it with green slime *shampoo*. Shampoo is *soap! Soap!* It's clean! All you have to do is get your brother's slugs—tell him I need them for a school project or something. I don't care what you say. And back up my story when I tell Tanja this afternoon."

Patsy shook her head. "I don't know, Aurora. I don't

56

think Tyler's gonna go for it. And what if he does and your plan doesn't work? Then what will you do?"

"Then I'll think of something else. Plan *B*."

"There isn't going to be any Plan *B*, Aurora. 'Cause if Plan A bombs, you're gonna get *killed*."

That afternoon, I told Tanja about the killer slugs. Jessica had refused to come. She didn't want anything to do with slugs—killer or otherwise. Patsy had refused, too, at first, but I'd finally talked her into it.

We found Tanja in the kitchen, trying to make German cookies with American ingredients. I guess it wasn't working too well because she kept tasting and frowning and then adding more stuff.

"Slugs?" she asked, dribbling lemon juice into the mixer bowl. "You mean those . . . how do you call them? Snails? Without the shells?"

I told her about the scientist and the poisonous slime and the scars and chills and fever. The part about dying seemed a bit much, so I left it out.

"Where did you hear this from?" Tanja asked suspiciously. "You are not only—how do you say?—pulling my arm?"

"Leg, Tanja. Pulling your leg. But I'm not. Really. We, um, saw a video about them at school. Didn't we, Patsy?"

"Umm," Patsy said. Tanja turned to look at her, and Patsy nodded like crazy. "Umm," she said again.

Tanja narrowed her eyes at me. "I am thinking . . . you are up to something."

I tried to look innocent. "Who, me?" I asked.

Later, in my room, I flopped down on my bed. "It worked!" I said. "She bought the whole thing!"

Patsy looked at me as though I had gone nuts.

"Well anyway, she didn't *not* believe it."

Patsy sighed and shook her head.

"The seed of doubt, Patsy. That's all we need."

"*Killed*, Aurora. You're gonna get *killed*."

ATTACK OF THE KILLER SLUGS

Shhh!"

Slowly, I pushed open the front door. I could hear Tanja's voice coming from somewhere in the back of the house.

"I think she's on the phone," Patsy whispered.

I nodded. There were no other voices, and Tanja was speaking German. She might be talking to someone in Germany or to another au pair. Either way, it could go on forever.

Perfect.

I motioned for Patsy to follow and, hugging Tyler's slug bowl, tiptoed upstairs. When I reached Tanja's room, I stopped. I had peeked in there, of course, but hadn't actually been inside. Not for the past two weeks. Not since it had been *my* room.

Patsy nudged me; we went in. The room seemed strange, now. Bigger, somehow. Definitely neater. Tanja didn't throw her clothes on the floor or leave her dresser drawers open or pile stuff on top of chairs. The room was full of unfamiliar things: unfamiliar photos on the dresser, unfamiliar knickknacks on the shelves. Two posters were stickpinned to the wall: a Snoopy poster and a poster of Lucy and Charlie Brown.

The room even smelled different now. It smelled like Tanja.

"Better hurry," Patsy whispered. "Tyler's gonna be here at four-thirty to pick up his slugs."

"I know."

I set the slug bowl on the floor. It was just a goldfish bowl full of dirt and damp leaves. A dishcloth stretched across the top of the bowl to keep the slugs inside. I slipped off the rubber band and the cloth.

"Come on, Patsy. It'll go faster if you help."

"No way. I shouldn't even be here. If Tyler finds out I even *suspected* you were going to do this, I'm dead."

"You're just chicken, like Jessica."

"Okay, so I'm chicken. I wouldn't touch those disgusting things for a million dollars."

They were pretty ugly, I had to admit. One had climbed up the glass and was sticking near the top of the bowl. It was fat and green and glistening. Underneath, where it clung to the bowl, it was the color of smoky glass. Two sets of tentacles waved in slow motion at the front end of the slug. It was at least five inches long.

I got an index card from my desk and tried to make the slug climb on. Its head—tentacles and all—disappeared

60

behind a slimy hood. I tried to slip the card between the slug and the glass, but the slug peeled off and flopped onto the leaves. I jabbed at it a couple of times with the card, but I couldn't pick it up.

"You're going to have to *touch* it," Patsy said, shuddering.

"Maybe I could use tweezers."

"No! Tyler says tweezers squish them."

I swallowed. Slowly, I reached into the bowl. Just as my finger was about to touch the slug's side, its head reappeared and its tentacles sprouted up from little budlike nubs.

"Yikes!" I yanked back my hand. I *couldn't*.

"Maybe this wasn't such a good idea, Aurora. Why don't we just forget it?"

"No!" Steeling myself, I reached down and grasped the slug between my index finger and thumb. It felt fleshy and slimy, sort of like a fat gummy worm dipped in raw egg white. I pried the slug from the glass, pushing down the queasy feeling in my stomach. I hurried across the room and dropped it onto Tanja's pillow. *Tried* to drop it. But the slug stuck to my fingers. I shook my hand hard until at last the slug flopped off.

Now my finger and thumb were sticky, as if I'd dipped them in glue.

Never mind. I'd wash them later.

The next slug was spotted like a leopard. I put it on the chair by the window. I tried to stick a slug to Tanja's Snoopy poster, but it kept falling off. I put it on top of

Tanja's TV. I thought about putting one on Tanja's toilet seat, but I was afraid it might fall in and drown. Tyler would murder me. I plugged the sink and put it there. I put the fifth slug, a bright yellow four-incher, on a picture frame on Tanja's dresser. It slithered down over the frame and waved its tentacles curiously. Could slugs understand photographs? I peered at the picture of Tanja and an older man and woman. Were those her parents?

"Psst! Aurora! Hurry up!"

I put the sixth slug on Tanja's camera case and the last one on the floor.

Now, for the slime.

They didn't have green slime shampoo at the supermarket where Mom usually shops, but that was okay, because Benjamin already uses green shampoo. It's slippery, like gel toothpaste, and it comes in a big green tube.

Perfect.

"Want to help with the slime?" I asked Patsy.

"No! I don't want anything to do with this, Aurora."

I opened Tanja's window a crack to make it look as if the slugs had come in that way. I squeezed the tube. A green blob spurted out on the shelf below the window. I dipped my finger in the blob and traced a trail up to the windowsill. Then I squeezed a line of shampoo to the first slug.

At first the lines came out blotchy and uneven, but after a while I got the hang of it. I began to make little curves and swirls in the lines, as if the slugs had wandered around before they got where I put them. I began to think of the slugs as having personalities: The spotted one was an

62

explorer slug who had checked out places all over the room before it wound up on the chair; the big green one was a wishy-washy slug who had gone around and around Tanja's bed in big, woozy circles; the little black one on the TV was a down-to-business sort of slug who knew exactly where he wanted to go and went directly there.

Trouble was, a couple of the slugs really *were* explorer slugs. They kept slithering away from where they were supposed to be, leaving their own silvery trails between themselves and my green slime trails. I kept picking them up and putting them back. I touched the green one's tentacles to get its attention; the tentacles shrank back, as if in surprise. "Stay," I said firmly. "Stay."

By the time I came to the last couple of slugs, I began to wish I hadn't gotten so carried away with slug personalities. The shampoo tube was nearly flat.

"Patsy, go to my parents' bathroom, would you, and find some more shampoo."

"No way I'm snooping around in your parents' bedroom. What if I get caught?"

I sighed. "Do I have to do *everything?*" I set down the shampoo tube. "At least you could stand guard."

Patsy shrugged. "Okay."

I rummaged through Mom's and Benjamin's bathroom cabinet with my unsticky hand. Aha! Benjamin had a spare tube. I ran out the door and almost bumped into Patsy, who was running in.

"Someone's here!"

"Who?"

"I don't know. A blue van just pulled in the driveway."

"Oh no! The mob. I didn't know they were coming."

"What should we do?"

"Uh . . ." I thought quickly. We could drop the plan, clean up everything really fast and put away the slugs. But Tyler would probably never let us borrow them again. This might be our only chance.

We'd make the best of it, I decided. If I could fool Tanja, I could fool the rest of the Mafia too. Maybe they'd *all* go back to Germany.

"You keep standing guard. I'm almost done."

I made the last two trails in a hurry. No fuss, no frills. I returned the explorer slugs to the ends of their slime trails, hid the slug bowl in my closet, put the old shampoo tube in my wastebasket, and put the new one back in Mom's and Benjamin's bathroom. I tried to wash off the slug slime, but it was really clingy stuff, like price tag glue. Finally, I managed to scrape most of it off with my thumbnail under warm running water.

By the time Patsy and I got downstairs, Gudrun and Elsa and the little kids were already in the family room. The au pairs were so wrapped up in talking about something that they hardly looked up.

I poured some juice for Patsy and me, and ransacked the cupboard until I came up with granola bars. Stewie, seeing me, toddled over. "Ror," he said.

"Hiya, Stewie, old buddy." I lifted him up on my lap. Ugh. He was wet.

I glanced at the mob. Still gabbing away. If Tanja didn't

discover the slugs soon, Tyler would come for them and Plan A would bomb.

"Hey, Stewie's diaper's wet," I called to Tanja.

"Pardon?" Tanja looked up. She looked worried.

"What's wrong?" I asked.

"Nothing. Just . . . a girl I met, an au pair who is being sent back to Sweden."

"How come?"

"Oh . . ." Tanja glanced at the other au pairs. "She was—how do you say it?—incompatible, I guess."

"What does that mean?"

Tanja shrugged. "I guess she just didn't . . . didn't work out."

Stewie toddled over to Tanja. "He's wet," I said.

"Oh, Stewie." Tanja bent to pick him up. She smiled wryly at the other au pairs. "My favorite job. I will soon return."

I peeked at Patsy, then concentrated hard on eating my granola bar as Tanja carried Stewie upstairs. I had left Tanja's door wide open, and a couple of slug trails could be seen from the hallway. I hoped Tanja looked in. I hoped the explorer slugs hadn't explored too far.

I waited. They must be at the top of the stairs by now. They must be at Stewie's door.

A scream.

The au pairs bolted for the stairs, followed by four-year-old Eliza and the twins, Ricky and Nicky. I grinned at Patsy; we followed. I pushed through the crowd just inside Tanja's door.

"Don't touch that slime!" I warned. "It may be poisonous."

"Poisonous?" Gudrun asked. "Slugs are not poisonous."

"These may be," I said. I found I couldn't look Gudrun in the eye as I continued. "Patsy and I saw a video about killer slugs the other day, didn't we, Patsy?"

Patsy grunted in a way that was supposed to mean yes.

"We told Tanja about them, don't you remember?"

Tanja looked as if a light had come on in her head. "*You* are responsible for this, Aurora, I know it."

"No I'm not. I told you, the killer slugs—"

"Killer *slugs?*" Gudrun, looking skeptical, bent to touch the slime.

"Don't touch that!" I said. "It'll burn right through your skin. You'll be scarred forever."

Gudrun stopped and gave me a long, hard look. I looked back as steadily as I could. Gudrun reached down and dipped a finger in the slime.

The doorbell rang.

There was a chorus of "I'll get it!" and "me go!" as the little kids thundered down the stairs.

"Hmm," Gudrun said, rubbing the slime between her fingers. She sniffed it.

My throat began to feel tight. "You better wash that off quick," I said. "Otherwise it might—"

"Aurora!" Eliza yelled.

"It Tyler!" Ricky yelled.

"He come up!" Nicky yelled.

Patsy let out a little squeak, darted into my bedroom and slammed the door.

Tyler! I raced to the railing and looked down.

It was Tyler. He was halfway up the stairs. He wasn't supposed to be here for another thirty minutes, at least.

"Stay right there, Tyler! I'm coming down!"

But Tyler was already at the top of the steps.

"Hey, Aurora," he said, "I've come for my—"

"Hiya, Tyler!" I ran to him and slapped him on the back. "How ya doin'?"

"Slugs," Tyler finished.

"Shampoo," Gudrun said.

"So!" Tanja was staring at me. "These are Tyler's slugs?"

"Shampoo! Look, in here." Gudrun bent to pick the empty tube out of the wastebasket.

My stomach sank.

"You let them out! You promised you wouldn't let them out!" Tyler pushed past the au pairs into Tanja's bedroom. "Luke, are you all right? Han? Leah?"

All three au pairs were glaring at me.

"Killer slugs, eh?" Elsa said.

"Poisonous slime, eh?" Gudrun added.

"I did know she had something up her cuff," Tanja said.

"Sleeve," I muttered. "Something up my sleeve. But I didn't, I . . ." I swallowed, trying to think up something to say, but my mind had gone blank. This couldn't be happening. This never happened with my plans. Even

67

when Jason Stoddard's ferret ate Amy Bates's goldfish at the pet show, it wasn't like *this*.

"I think you had better leave us now," Gudrun said. "We have to clean up this mess."

"You are in big trouble, Aurora," Tanja put in. "*Very* big."

When Tanja said *very* it sounded like *wery*, but I didn't point this out. I couldn't think what to do, with the whole mob glaring at me and the minimob gaping and Tyler still calling his slugs. I turned and headed for my room.

"Big trouble," I heard Ricky say in an awed voice. "*Wery* big."

BIG TROUBLE

I was waiting for the big trouble to start.

Patsy and I had holed up in my room with the door shut until we'd heard Tyler leave. Then Patsy ran for home. I went down to the living room with a book. I knew I'd better not go anywhere, but I wanted to be as far from the mob as possible.

Upstairs, they were moving around in Tanja's room. I heard talking and a scrubbing sound and the sound of running water. I wondered why they didn't make *me* clean up. Maybe they didn't trust me. I heard the little kids galloping through the hallway and pounding up and down the stairs. Every so often they poked their heads into the living room to stare at me, and one of them whispered, "Big trouble."

After a while I heard the au pairs coming downstairs. I scooted to a corner of the couch where they couldn't see me and hunched over my book. I'd never had so many people mad at me all at once. It was kind of scary.

But no one came in. Gudrun and Elsa left with their kids, and before long I heard Tanja in the kitchen fixing dinner.

She was going to do something—I knew it. Probably tell, like she did on Halloween.

She didn't tell at dinner. Benjamin made a big fuss over the German soup Tanja had made—a starchy, lumpy glop, about as appetizing as paste. I stared down into my bowl and tried to figure out what was floating in it. Lentils. Strange, foreign noodles. Other suspicious-looking things that I didn't even want to *think* about. I had no intention of eating it, but I decided not to complain. Right now, I didn't want to call attention to myself. I reached for some apple slices and a handful of crackers.

When Mom asked Tanja how her day had been, I held my breath, but Tanja didn't even mention the slugs. Amazing. But she'd probably tell later.

Stewie jabbed his spoon at me. "Bik tubble," he said.

"What's this? Bubble?" Mom asked, turning to me.

"Uh, I . . ."

"Does he mean bubble gum?" Benjamin asked. "I hope it was sugarless, Aurora. You know what that sugary stuff does to your teeth."

"Uh, yeah," I said, glancing sideways at Tanja. She was looking down at her soup. "I mean, no. I wasn't chewing bubble gum with sugar."

Benjamin seemed satisfied. "We don't encourage sugary

70

snacks around our house," he said to Tanja. "Especially sticky things like bubble gum and taffy. But, of course, you remember that from Halloween."

I remembered. Benjamin had gone through our trick or treat bags, taking out all the sticky stuff.

I waited for Tanja to say something about the "tubble," but she just kept on eating her soup.

Why didn't she say something? Was she waiting until I went to bed? Had she forgiven me and decided to do nothing? Or . . . was the mob planning some secret revenge of its own?

Suddenly suspicious, I peered at the saltshaker. It wasn't the kind with a lid. I'd never noticed that before. So that was safe. The mob couldn't have gotten hold of a dribble glass on such short notice, but I picked up my glass and checked it for holes anyway.

"Aurora, have you tried Tanja's soup?" Mom asked.

No holes.

"This soup is delicious," Benjamin said. "Give it a try, Aurora."

I stared at my soup. Suddenly, it looked worse than unappetizing. It looked . . . sinister. What *were* those mysterious lumps and specks, those unidentified floating objects? All at once it struck me that Tanja could have put *anything* in there. She could have poisoned it, even.

No, she wouldn't do that. But the mob . . . they might have put her up to it. They wouldn't poison everybody's soup, of course. Nobody else seemed to be choking or gagging—although they might just be trying to be polite.

But Tanja had *served* the soup too. She could have poisoned only mine. That would be trouble, for sure.

No. Tanja wouldn't do that.

Would she?

"Aurora." Mom's voice sounded ominous. "Eat your soup."

"It's . . . disgusting," I said under my breath.

"Aurora!" Mom glared.

"Well, it is."

"You can't possibly know what it tastes like unless you try it," Benjamin said in his I'm-trying-very-hard-to-be-reasonable voice.

"Yes I can. I can *see* how it tastes."

"Aurora, that is rude," Mom said. "Tanja worked hard on this soup, and it's delicious. If you can't be civilized and at least try it, you'd better go up to your room."

Everyone was staring at me, except for Tanja, who was looking into her soup bowl as if she could read her fortune in the lentils.

She was up to something. But what?

"'Scuse me," I mumbled, and got up to leave.

But—the thought came to me halfway up the stairs—was it safe in my room? The mob had been upstairs for a long time this afternoon. They might have booby trapped my room. Maybe that's why they didn't want me up there cleaning. Or maybe Tanja was going to sneak in there later, when I was asleep.

Spiders. Tabasco sauce. Yarn and honey. There were a thousand things she might do.

My bedroom door was partway open. I looked up. No bucket. Slowly, I stepped inside.

My room still looked pretty much the way I'd left it. Although it was kind of hard to tell. Yesterday's school clothes lay in a pile upon the floor. Socks and sweaters spilled over the tops of my dresser drawers. I never can manage to get them all the way shut. I hadn't made my bed this morning; the covers made a lumpy heap.

I looked around for the obvious things: fake dog doo, a rubber scorpion, something like that.

Nothing.

Carefully, I shook out the clothes on the floor before putting them in my hamper. I pawed through my dresser drawers, through the sheets and blankets on my bed, looking for snakes, spiders, ice cubes, peanut butter, or any other nasty surprises the mob might have left.

Nothing.

I looked behind the curtains and under my bed. I searched my closet and checked my shoes for bubble gum. I scraped the bristles of my hairbrush with my fingernails.

No peanut butter.

At last I washed my face and brushed my teeth—but not before checking the toothpaste, toothbrush, and soap.

Then I barricaded myself inside my room. I locked the door and leaned my chair against it, jamming the chair back under the knob the way I'd seen someone do it on TV. After that, I stuffed some underwear into the crack beneath the door.

73

"Come and get me now," I muttered. "I'd like to see you try."

Determined to stay awake all night, I crawled into bed with a book. But I couldn't read. My thoughts kept interrupting.

What was the big trouble? And when would it strike?

PLAN B

It didn't strike that night. I fell asleep sitting up, and when I woke my neck was sore, but nothing worse had happened.

Why not? All the next day, I couldn't stop wondering. Was Tanja waiting for the right moment to tell? Was she going to blackmail me? Was she trying to make me suffer in suspense?

She *couldn't* just be being nice—could she?

The thought made me feel uncomfortable, somehow.

No. Couldn't be.

But the trouble didn't strike that day. And after dinner, Mom and I went bowling.

I couldn't believe it. We actually went.

I did terrible at first. The ball felt all wobbly in my hands, and half the time it sort of limped across the alley and dribbled into the gutter at the last minute. Mom didn't make any comments, which was a good thing. It was her fault, anyway. If she'd stood up to Benjamin we wouldn't have stopped bowling in the first place, and I wouldn't have gotten so rusty.

But by the second game, it all started coming back to me. I got a spare on the first frame, and a strike right after.

Mom wasn't doing so hot, though, so I gave her some pointers. "You're twisting your arm back behind you," I said. "Aim for the third mark."

After that, she got better.

It began to feel like the old days, when I used to give her advice all the time. I told her what clothes she looked best in, and when she had lipstick on her teeth. I told her which boyfriends were nice and which weren't. Benjamin was actually the nicest one, but I wish she hadn't married him. I told her not to. It's not that he's a wicked stepfather or anything like that—except he's always hogging Mom's attention and winning her over to his side. And that health food thing of his: he's a fanatic. I mean really off the deep end.

But the thing I noticed first was, he's so . . . parenty. He can hardly watch a movie—even a funny one—without making a moral out of it. "See, Aurora, that's what happens when you don't tell the truth," he'll say. Or, "That's why you should never smoke."

The only times I've seen him unparenty are sometimes with Mom. She knows just how to tease him so he gets flustered in the middle of a lecture on Why Cupboards Should Never Be Left Open, or—his all-time favorite— The Dangers of Sticky Taffy. "Especially for people who have lettuce stuck between their teeth," Mom says—or something like that—and he all of a sudden looks less like a big parenty adult than a little kid caught chewing gum at school. Then she runs over and kisses him and his bald spot turns pink.

After bowling that night, we went out for frozen yogurt. Everything was fine until Mom asked what was wrong between Tanja and me. "It's been over two weeks, now," she said. "I was sure you and Tanja would be great friends by now. This just . . . doesn't seem like you, Aurora."

All of a sudden my yogurt tasted sour.

"What did she tell you?" I said. I *knew* she would tell.

"She hasn't said anything. She doesn't need to. I can see there's a problem and I wish . . . I don't know, Aurora. Can you tell me what's the matter?"

I shrugged.

Tanja hadn't told. Not yet, anyway. I almost wished she had. It felt strange sitting here, with Mom not knowing about that. . . .

Can you tell me what's the matter? she had asked. I'd already told her I didn't want a nanny bossing me around, but that wasn't the whole thing. I'd told her I wanted her to be there when I got home after school, but that wasn't quite all of it, either. The heart of it was stuck like a splinter deep down in a place where it would hurt to dig it out. "I don't know. Tanja just doesn't like me, that's all. Can't we send her back to Germany?"

"Honey, from what I've seen, you haven't given her a chance to like you. And I'd like to know why. You don't think that . . . I don't know . . . that you're not as precious

77

to me as always, or something silly like that? Because if you do—"

"No! I don't think that! Why would I think that?" I slouched down in my seat and crossed my arms, not looking at her.

Mom reached across the table and squeezed my hand. "Honey . . ." I felt the tears welling up behind my eyes. I waited for Mom to say it, say the thing she used to say all the time: You're my specialest girl in the whole wide world.

But then one of Benjamin's patients came in and started talking to Mom, and by the time he stopped talking we had to go. And after that we couldn't get back to where we'd been.

And a memory was nagging at me, an echo of something Tanja had said yesterday.

Incompatible. Didn't work out.

Through the dull ache in my chest I felt the first faint glimmerings of another brilliant scheme: Plan *B*.

SUPER
SLEUTH

*F*irst thing the next morning, I was ready. Plan *B*, into
action! I waited for exactly the right moment, when
Benjamin and Mom had left for work and Tanja was
downstairs feeding Stewie. Then I tiptoed into Benjamin's
and Mom's bedroom and found Mrs. Stephanus's phone
number in the address book they kept in their nightstand.

I took a deep breath, then dialed.

"Hello?" It was Mrs. Stephanus.

"Hi. This is Aurora. Aurora MacKenzie."

"Oh. Hello, Aurora."

"I don't think Tanja is working out," I said.

There was a pause.

"Mrs. Stephanus? Did you hear me?"

"Yes, Aurora. I heard."

"I wouldn't have called unless it was really serious." I
had practiced that line. I had practiced this whole phone

conversation, trying to imagine what Mrs. Stephanus would say and figuring out what to say back.

"Tanja and I are just . . . incompatible," I said. That was the word Tanja had used when she'd told about the au pair who was sent back to Sweden. Incompatible.

"I see," Mrs. Stephanus said. Another pause. I imagined her creasing her forehead and peering down from over her glasses, the way she had at the airport. "Aurora," she asked, "have you talked to your mother about this?"

"Well, yeah, I tried to talk to her but . . . but she just doesn't understand. I think she's too busy worrying about her job or something. But I thought with you being in charge of the au pairs and all, you might have had this kind of thing happen before. I mean, having to send one back."

"Ah," Mrs. Stephanus said.

There were more pauses than talk in this conversation, I thought.

"Aurora, why don't I just talk to your mother and we'll see if we can't work this out. I'll call her this evening and—"

"No! She'll kil—I mean," I said quickly, "she doesn't need to know I called. I just wanted you to know that Tanja and I are—you know—incompatible."

Mrs. Stephanus sighed. "What exactly do you mean by incompatible, Aurora?"

"Well, she just doesn't like me, that's all."

"How do you know?"

"Well, the way she acts."

80

"You're going to have to be more specific than that."

"Um, she doesn't do things for me anymore."

"What things?"

"She used to fix me breakfast and"—I thought about mentioning the brownies and decided against it—"and stuff. She used to make my bed. She used to meet me at the door when I came home from school. Now she hardly even *talks* to me anymore."

"Tanja's duties don't include picking up after you," Mrs. Stephanus said. "I'm sure your mother told you that. As for the climate of general . . . unfriendliness . . . usually it takes two to dance *that* tango."

"What do you mean?"

"Let me put it this way, Aurora. Usually when two people aren't getting along, both of them had something to do with it. Have you done anything to alienate Tanja?"

"Uh, no. Not . . . really."

"Not . . . really?"

"Well . . ." I didn't think Tanja had told Mom and Benjamin about the brownies or the killer slugs. Not yet. But had she told Mrs. Stephanus? And had Mom told Mrs. Stephanus about the trick-or-treating? I had no way of knowing. "Just normal stuff, you know. Just stuff everybody does. We're incompatible, that's all there is to it."

"Ah," Mrs. Stephanus said again.

I didn't like the sound of that "ah." I had thought that "incompatible" would be enough. I felt Plan *B* slipping away from me, the way everything else had done.

"What about that other au pair I heard about, the one who was sent back to Sweden?" I asked. "She was incompatible too."

"That was an entirely different situation, where the grievances were well documented, and—"

"What does 'well documented' mean?"

"In writing. It was completely different, Aurora. Look, why don't you try talking to your mother again? I'm sure you can work this out. . . ."

But I wasn't listening anymore. *In writing.* I felt the unmistakable, back-of-the-neck prickling sensation of another idea coming on.

"Aurora? Can you do that? Try talking to your mother again?"

"I guess so. Ah, thanks, Mrs. Stephanus."

Sigh. "You're welcome, Aurora."

That's *it!* I slammed down the phone and did a little dance. Plan C, coming up!

I was Sherlock Holmes! I was Harriet the Spy! No—I was Aurora Jane MacKenzie, Super Sleuth!

Tanja had to goof up sometime, and when she did, I would be ready. It would be "in writing." I would document it like crazy.

I rummaged through my desk drawer for my purple spiral notebook, the one I'd used for brainstorming, and wrote "Spy Notebook" in black felt pen on the cover.

Hmm. Spies don't usually go around advertising that

they're spies. I blacked out "Spy Notebook" and wrote beneath it, "Research."

That would do. That would do quite nicely.

The trouble with spying, I discovered, is you have to get close to hear the good stuff—but no one wants to talk about the good stuff when you're close enough to hear.

The trouble with spying on Tanja was that half the time I couldn't understand *any* of the stuff she was talking about—no matter how close I got. Because when she was with the mob, they all spoke German.

If it hadn't been for Holly and the heating vent, I don't know what I would have done.

Holly was a new au pair from England. She'd moved in with the family next door to Gudrun and had become good friends with the rest of the mob. But Holly didn't speak German, so whenever she was there, they all switched to English.

The heating vent was on the floor in my room. It connected up to all the other heating vents in the house, but the closest one was in Tanja's room. On evenings when the au pairs met at our house—which they did a lot, because Tanja had a big room with a TV—I could press my ear against the vent and hear their faint, tinny-sounding voices.

Listening at the heating vent, I got more ammunition in the last two weeks of November than I could have gotten any other way in a year.

"Stewie is making me crazy!" Tanja said one night after dinner.

Hates Stewie, I wrote.

"I mean, I do love him, but he is never for one minute staying still. Today he did take a stick of butter and scrub the kitchen wall with it? And when I was cleaning up that, he did throw his mother's shoes into the toilet?"

Lets Stewie destroy property, like walls, shoes, I wrote. *Clogs toilets.*

"And when I was cleaning up for that, he tried to play piano with his feet and did slip and bump his head. And now he does have a lump."

Does not watch carefully. Endangers Stewie's life: falling off piano, bump on head, etc. Brain damage? I wrote.

Sometimes the au pairs talked about parties they had been to and boys they knew. Elsa was the only one who had a real boyfriend in Oregon. His name was Henry, and he lived by himself in a house halfway up Mount Hood. He had this old, beat-up car that broke down a lot. Sometimes, when his car broke down, the au pairs all went up together to visit him and bring him groceries, because Elsa wasn't allowed to go there alone.

Boy crazy, I wrote. *Party animal.*

I told Patsy about the heating vent, and naturally she had to come try it. Jessica was too busy to come; lately, it seemed like she was always shopping for Amsterdam or doing something else too important for us.

Patsy and I lay on the floor, our ears pressed to the vent,

our heads so close together I couldn't look at her without going cross-eyed. We had to concentrate hard on the voices, like listening to an old-fashioned radio program. Sometimes we couldn't help giggling. We'd scramble to the far side of my room and crack up with our hands clapped over our mouths.

Later, we practiced talking with a German accent, saying *w* for *v*, and *tch* for *j*, and making our sentences sound like questions. "I am going in the wan to get some wery waluable wideotapes?" we would say. And, "Tcholly Tchimmy Tchonson tchayvalks in the tchungle?"

I spied in other ways besides the heating vent. Like getting to know Tanja's routine. I knew for a fact that Tanja could hear the mail truck coming a mile away. How else could she manage to be waiting at the mailbox every time the truck came? Then, if there were letters from Germany, she would be incommunicado for fifteen minutes— minimum. Half an hour, if there were pictures. An earthquake could level the house, but if Tanja had mail from Germany, she wouldn't budge. I considered confiscating a letter to see if I could find more evidence for my notebook, but I decided against it. Mail tampering is a federal crime. Besides, all the letters were written in German.

I also knew that if you answered the phone and called, "It's Germany!" Tanja would get to a phone—no matter where she'd been or what she'd been doing—in two seconds flat. She spent so much time on the phone—

talking to Germany or just to Oregon—that Benjamin began muttering about *his* calls not coming through. Two days later, Tanja got her own private phone line.

The whole time I was spying, I kept hoping to hear something about the big trouble I was supposed to be in. I couldn't believe I had gotten off scot-free. So when I heard my name through the heating vent one night, I really listened hard.

". . . do not think she does like me," Tanja was saying.

"She's a brat," Elsa said. "You can't help how she is."

I sat up fast. I felt stung, as if I'd been slapped. I hadn't expected that Elsa would like me very much, but to hear it like this, straight out. . . .

I stared down at the heating vent. Faraway, metallic-sounding bits of talk floated up to my ears.

Did I really want to hear this? Or not?

". . . rude girl . . ."

". . . too big for her trousers . . ."

". . . think I do understand how she must feel . . ."

Tanja's voice. I bent down to the vent.

". . . because when my old cat died, the one that I did love since I was a baby, and my parents bought for me a new kitten, I was for a while angry at the kitten."

"Aurora has no cat," Elsa said.

"Yes, but . . . I am in a way doing what her mother used to do, before she did go for her job. And maybe Aurora would prefer that her mother still does this, like before."

"You mean it's like you're taking Aurora's mother's place?" Holly's voice.

"No, no, I am not! But maybe she does see it this way, that if I do not come, her mother will be staying home."

"That isn't your fault," Gudrun said. "You just do the job they asked you."

"Yes, I know, but . . ."

"Oh, poor Aurora," Elsa said mockingly.

Tanja laughed. "Yes, but . . . it is a little bit the same, I think . . ." she said, and then the furnace came on, and its soft whooshing sound drowned out the voices.

Slowly, I pushed away from the vent. There was a lump inside my throat, and no matter how hard I swallowed, I couldn't push it down.

COOTIES

Ammunition, I thought, thumbing through my purple notebook. Do I have enough?

Reading back through the pages, I felt sort of let down. *Hates Stewie* didn't say very much. *Lets Stewie destroy property, like wall, shoes* seemed kind of flimsy, even when I wrote down exactly what Stewie had done. *Boy crazy. Party animal* sounded dumb.

I had thought this plan would be easy, but here it was the last day of November—Tanja had been here exactly one month—and what did I have? Nothing.

The thing was, Tanja never seemed to do anything wrong. I mean really wrong. Sure, she put Stewie in the playpen more than Mom did. And lots of times when he was out, he got into things. And once, when he pulled the toaster cord and almost got creamed when the toaster came crashing down, she spanked him. I wrote everything down, of course. But reading it in my notebook, I felt kind of strange. I can't describe it, exactly. It was like, you could see *me* behind the words, trying to twist them around to make Tanja look bad. Which made me feel . . . I don't know. Funny. Not good. Not the way I used to feel when I was doing one of my plans.

I sighed and closed my notebook. I needed something big. Something bad. Like a deep, dark secret Tanja was keeping because it was too disgraceful to tell. I needed . . . what did you call that?

A skeleton. A skeleton in the closet. I needed to find one of those.

I stuffed my notebook under my mattress. Oh, well. Back to the heating vent again.

The next day, Sunday, I heard more giggling than usual from Tanja's room. The whole mob was in there, and I was alone in the house with them because Benjamin had gone golfing and Mom had taken Stewie to the store.

I pressed my ear to the vent. Music. Talking. More giggling. Every so often I heard a high, whirring click, the sound Tanja's camera made.

All at once there was a knocking at my door.

"Aurora?" Tanja's voice. "May I come in?"

I leaped to my feet, grabbed a comic book from my dresser, and dove onto my bed, which *refused* to stop bouncing even as the door opened. I pretended to read the comics.

"Aurora, would you do for us a favor? Would you take a photograph of us in our outfits?"

"What outf—" I began, then stopped, looking up.

Tanja looked weird. Her face seemed really pale, and her hair poofed out around her head. Her lips were bright red, her eyes had thick dark lines around them, and there was a black beauty mark near her mouth. She looked like a poster I'd once seen of an old-time movie star, Marilyn Monroe.

"Are you . . . all right?" I asked.

Tanja laughed. "We are—how do you say it?—dressing up. And we do need someone to photograph us together."

I shrugged. "Okay." I followed Tanja into her room, wondering how her tight black dress stayed where it was supposed to stay without straps or sleeves or anything else to hold it up.

Elsa and Gudrun and Holly had outfits too—dresses with plunging necklines and skinny shoulder straps and slits that bared their legs. Jewelry glittered at their wrists and throats. Perfume hung thick as chalk dust in the air.

"Are you . . . going someplace?" I asked.

"No! Not like this!" Laughing, Tanja picked up her camera from the bed. "This is a . . . a joke on our friends in Stuttgart. We are telling them that this is how American girls do look, that this is how we do look now, in America. And so we rented these outfits and we do need this photograph to send home to them."

Tanja showed me where to look through the camera and which button to press. The other three au pairs crowded together, whispering and giggling. With all that black goop around their eyes, they looked like a family of raccoons.

Tanja slipped in beside Elsa. "Ready."

Just as I pressed the shutter, Tanja held up two fingers in a cootie sign behind Elsa. *Click!* "Cooties," Tanja said.

"No fair!" Elsa complained. "Aurora, do another one."

This time, Gudrun made cooties behind Elsa, and Holly made cooties behind Gudrun. *Click!* "Stop it, all of you!" Elsa said. "Do another one."

There was a tangle of arms as everyone tried to put cooties on everyone else. *Click!*

"Just one!" Elsa pleaded. "Just one with no cooties on anybody."

"You are no fun," Gudrun said.

But then they all posed, smiling, and for a moment nobody made cooties. I quickly pressed the shutter. *Click!*

"All right, I am *finished*," Gudrun said. "This stupid bra is cutting off the blood to my head."

The au pairs drifted apart in a rustling cloud of giggles and perfume.

"Wait, Gudrun?" Tanja said. "Would you take one of Aurora and me?"

Me? Why did she want one of me?

But Gudrun already had the camera. Tanja put her arm around me. "Say 'cheese,'" she said. Mixed in with the perfume, I could smell the smell that was only Tanja's. I felt the warmth of Tanja's side against my side, the warmth of Tanja's arm across my back. Just as Gudrun squeezed the shutter, I thrust up my arm and stuck two fingers behind Tanja's head.

Click!

"Cooties!" I said.

Tanja grinned. I leaned away and saw Tanja's hand up behind me. "Cooties, yourself!"

I laughed and gave Tanja a little shove. Tanja laughed and gave me a little squeeze. "Here," Tanja said. "Maybe you would like to try some of these?"

She held out a tin of cookies. The tin had foreign writing on it; it must have been from Stuttgart. But the cookies looked pretty good.

I reached for one, then stopped. "Mom and Benjamin don't want you to give me sweets," I said. I watched carefully to see what Tanja would do.

"Well . . ." Tanja shrugged. "Maybe just this one time?"

I hesitated, then picked one. It was sweet and light and buttery.

"Have some more," Tanja said. "My sister did send me these from Stuttgart because she knew that I was homesick."

Homesick? I looked up to see what homesick looked like. But Tanja had joined the others in the corner by her bed; they were talking and laughing and changing their clothes. I stood there a moment, not knowing what to do. No one had told me to leave. Actually, to my amazement, I didn't really *want* to leave.

"Let's ask Aurora," Tanja was saying.

"Ask me what?"

"Elsa thinks my niece, Helga, has a resemblance with you. She is younger, of course, but see what you do think."

Tanja took a fat photo album off a shelf and set it down on her table. She flipped through the pages, which were covered with photographs, all neatly labeled in German. She pointed to a picture of a dark-haired girl about seven years old. "Helga," and a date, were written just below. Helga's arms were crossed. She glared up at me.

"Perhaps it is her eyes?" Tanja said.

I looked at Helga's eyes. They were blue, not greenish brown like mine. Still, there was something about them, something . . .

"She looks the way I *feel* sometimes," I said.

Tanja bent closer to the picture. "Maybe that is it," she said slowly. "You and Helga, you are of the same spirit. You both have—what is that word I did hear somebody say? Spunk. You are not a limp *spätzle* noodle, like me."

Spunk. Was that how Tanja thought of me? I liked the sound of it. I've got spunk, I said to myself.

Tanja flipped through the pages of her album, showing me pictures of her mother and her father and her three older sisters. She pointed out two cats: the cat she had now, and her old cat that had died.

"She was the best cat," Tanja said. "She did curl up on my feet to keep them warm at night. She did talk to me when I woke up. . . ." Then she looked at me in a funny sort of way and said, "But now I love my new cat too."

"Oh," I mumbled, feeling my face go all hot, keeping my eyes zeroed in on the album.

Then Elsa said something to Tanja, and Tanja moved to where the au pairs were clustered around the bed. But I kept turning the pages of the album. I had never thought much about Tanja's family, and yet there they all were. Tanja's mother and her father and her three older sisters. Her two cats. Her niece who had spunk.

All at once I was struck by Tanja's courage—leaving her family and friends and everything she had known all her life, to come to a place where no one knew her and she could hardly speak the language without people making fun.

Then something else caught my eye: Another picture, a picture of myself, in my wolf man mask at the airport. I was half-in, half-out of the picture; Tanja must not have held the camera straight when she'd taken it.

But wait—Tanja hadn't taken that picture. The only person who could have was Mrs. Stephanus, when Tanja had turned to meet me for the first time, and I'd yelled, "Yah!" and made Tanja drop all her things.

I ran my fingers across the photograph, so neatly tucked into its black corner-holders, so carefully labeled with my own name and the date. As if it meant something to Tanja. As if it were important to her, somehow.

I turned the page, and my eye caught on another picture from when Tanja first came: A picture of me, Mom, Benjamin, Stewie, and Tanja. My face looked pale; you could barely see my wolf man makeup. I remembered how I had felt that night—left out, as if everybody else belonged to a private club I wasn't allowed to join.

Had that been only a month ago? Yeah, that was right. Only a month. But it sure felt longer than that.

Underneath the photo there was writing that said, *"meine amerikanische Familie." Familie* must be "family" in German. *Amerikanische* probably meant "American." Did *meine* mean "my?"

My American family.

And strangely, I didn't mind Tanja calling my family her own. Because in the picture we did look like a family. Everyone was smiling. Mom's hand rested on my shoulder, which I didn't remember at all.

"Aurora?"

Tanja, dressed again in jeans and a T-shirt, came toward me, holding something in her hand.

"My sister gave me some of these in the box she did send. It is *Kinderschokolade*, my favorite in the world."

Chocolate. My mouth began to water. But I hesitated, remembering how Tanja had promised Benjamin not to let me have candy, thinking about what good ammunition this would make for my notebook. *Offered me chocolate,* I would write. *But I turned it down.*

"You know I'm not allowed. . . ." I began, and then stopped. Tanja, holding out the chocolate, looked dead into my eyes. She's *trusting* me, I realized with a jolt.

"Well . . ." I shrugged. "Okay."

Germans make good chocolate, too, I discovered. Three good things: good chocolate, and good cookies, and good pancakes.

But they can *keep* their soup.

I licked my fingers, thinking about using the chocolate as ammunition for my notebook. I could still do it.

But on the other hand, chocolate wasn't as bad as taffy or gum with sugar. It wasn't much of a skeleton at all. So maybe I'd leave it out.

Just this one time. What difference would it make?

SKELETON IN THE CLOSET

I wasn't expecting the skeleton when it came. It happened the very next day, when I was walking up the driveway after school and Tanja pulled up in the van. She had the whole mob with her, plus the minimob. The garage door rumbled open and the van drove in, but not all the way in, because Stewie's tricycle blocked the way.

Kids and au pairs came pouring out, carrying stuffed animals and shopping bags and diaper bags. Tanja cut the engine and came around to open the rear van door. She smiled at me and asked if I had my key.

I nodded and headed through the garage to the door to the house.

Just as I got there, I heard the rumble. I turned to look. The garage door was coming down. It was going to hit the van.

I stared. I knew I should do something, but I couldn't make myself move. No one else moved, either, until—

"Stewie!" Tanja cried. Then Tanja and Holly raced for the front of the van. Stewie was standing on the front seat, holding the garage door opener.

Boom! The garage door hit down on the roof of the van.

Tanja flung open the van door, leaped inside, and grabbed the door opener from Stewie. The door made a funny buzzing noise like a toaster when the toast is hung up inside. It didn't budge.

"It will not go up!" Tanja wailed. *"Sie ist kaputt!"*

Stewie started crying. Everybody crowded around the car door, all talking at the same time.

". . . thought he was still strapped in . . ."

". . . door go boom . . ."

". . . I did take off his strap . . ."

". . . thought he was outside the van . . ."

". . . crash! . . ."

". . . slam! Kabash! . . ."

". . . another button, inside the garage . . ."

". . . over there, where Aurora was standing . . ."

All at once, everyone was looking at me. Accusingly, I thought.

"I didn't do it," I said. "I was just—"

"Just *push* it," Gudrun said.

I pushed. The garage door made the same funny buzzing noise but still didn't budge.

"I have to move it!" Tanja's eyes looked scared and wild. The engine roared to life. "They will kill me to find it here—"

98

"You had better wait," Gudrun said. "You will make it worse."

But the van was creeping forward. Gudrun sprang to move Stewie's tricycle out of the way; the other au pairs shooed the little kids back. The garage door scraped along the van roof, hit down on the bumper, scraped along the top of the bumper, and crashed to the ground.

We all rushed for the rear of the van to check out the damage. I got a toehold on a corner of the bumper and pulled myself up. The roof wasn't too bad, considering. There was a tiny dent where the door had first hit and thin, white scratches between the dent and the rear of the van.

"They will kill me," Tanja said. "They will send me back to Germany."

"It wasn't your fault," Holly said. "Stewie did it."

"But I was responsible to watch him."

"*Nobody* could be watching Stewie all the time," Elsa said. "He is never stopping."

"Oh, I wish I did not move the van," Tanja said, and bit her lip.

All at once, I felt sorry for Tanja. She would have to tell Mom and Benjamin what had happened. For sure they wouldn't kill her, and they probably wouldn't send her back to Germany—not just for this. But they wouldn't be happy about it. Not at all.

"They do have insurance to pay for these accidents," Gudrun said. "Just tell them what happened and it will be all right."

"Maybe you should wait until a proper time to tell them of this?" Elsa suggested. "When they are having good feelings about you?"

"Maybe they won't see it," Holly said.

"I can't see it," Elsa said, standing on tiptoe. "Except if I get up on this fender."

"No, you must tell, but you can wait for a good time. Then, tell it in your own way, so it does not sound . . ." Gudrun stopped and looked at me. Suddenly, they were *all* looking at me.

I tried to look innocent, but I felt . . . I don't know . . . powerful.

Big trouble. But not for me.

"Aurora, I do think you should let Tanja tell about this?" Gudrun said. "When she does feel the time is right?"

"You can't trust her," Elsa said to Gudrun. Then, to me, "If you tell about this, we will tell about the slugs. You will be in big trouble, for certain."

Something hardened inside me. I hadn't felt like telling before, not really. But now . . .

"I won't say a word," I said.

Elsa gave me a long look. "You better not."

I remembered what Elsa had called me before. A brat, she had said.

So I *wouldn't* say a word. But boy, was I going to write!

THE GREAT
ESCAPE

Somehow, I let three days go by without calling Mrs. Stephanus. I was *going* to do it. I definitely was. It was just . . . every time I picked up the phone to call her, I didn't feel like it.

Anyway, things had been going okay lately. Mom and I had gone bowling again—it was the fourth time since Tanja had come—and that was pretty fun. I still wished Mom hadn't gone back to work. I wished she and Benjamin hadn't gotten together and taken over everything.

But things were going okay.

"Did you tell Mrs. Stephanus yet?" Patsy asked Friday after school. "About the accident?"

"No," I said. "I don't know, I just—"

"If you're going to do it, you better do it soon," Jessica said. "Someone's bound to notice that scratch. And if Tanja tells about the van on her own, that notebook of yours is worthless."

"I know that already; you don't have to tell me," I said, feeling cross. "I'll take it to a copying machine this afternoon. In case the original gets lost. Tanja's taking Stewie and me to the mall, and I can sneak my notebook inside my jacket."

"You know, Aurora," Patsy said, "you don't *have* to do this. You can just stop now if you want to."

I kicked at a pebble on the sidewalk. I knew I didn't have to. I'd been thinking about that a lot. I did still want Mom to stay home, but I didn't want to do anything . . . mean . . . to Tanja.

"Yeah, it's good to admit it when you're wrong," Jessica said. "I knew all along you were wrong about Tanja."

"I'm not *wrong*, all right? I just . . . it's hard to get stuff copied. I'll do it today at the mall."

"Okay, Aurora." Jessica looked smug. "Whatever you say."

Halfway to the mall, I remembered my purple notebook. Oh, great. I'd left it at home. But where? I remembered taking the notebook out of my room and putting it on the kitchen table. After that, Stewie's stroller had gotten stuck in the open position and wouldn't fit in the van so I pushed it shut while Tanja held it steady. Then Stewie spilled juice all over the front of his overalls and Tanja had to change him. I had stuffed diapers and plastic pants and bottles and teething cookies into Stewie's diaper bag. Then Tanja

102

couldn't remember where she'd left her keys. I got Stewie into his coat and his red pompon hat while Tanja searched.

So the notebook was probably still out there in plain sight on the kitchen table.

I shifted uneasily in the van seat. What if Mom and Benjamin got home before we did and found it there?

They wouldn't read it, would they? It was private.

Then Stewie dropped his bear-bear and started to cry, and I reached behind my seat to pick it up, and Tanja asked what Benjamin would like for Christmas, and the notebook faded to a niggling itch at the back of my mind.

It was only the first week in December, but the Christmas shopping season was going full blast, so it took forever to find a parking place. When we finally did, it was way out in the boonies. Tanja gave Stewie some pennies to give to the Salvation Army Santa outside Sears, but Stewie tried to eat them so she had to fish them out of his mouth. We plunged into the warm, noisy, popcorn-smelling store and squeezed in with the crowd in the aisles.

Stewie didn't want to stay strapped in his stroller. "Up," he kept saying, which meant he wanted someone to lift him up out of the stroller, and then put him down so he could walk. When we reached the endless, winding line for pictures with Santa, Tanja let him out. I took him on a scouting expedition through the mall while Tanja held our place. When at last our turn came, Tanja made me get in the picture too. "This one is for your parents," she said. "They will want you in it."

"I *refuse* to sit on Santa's lap," I said.

"Then stand beside him, won't you please?"

"If any of my friends ever see this I'm *dead*," I muttered as I posed with Stewie and Santa.

"Say 'cheese,'" Tanja said.

"Limburger!"

Then Tanja made us pose again. "This one is for me," she said.

After we picked up our Polaroids, we moved on to Nordstrom's where Tanja shopped for Christmas presents and I took Stewie on more scouting expeditions. Stewie loved escalators; we rode up and down nine times.

We were on our way out when we heard carolers singing. Tanja made for the sound like a marble rolling downhill. It was a high school choir. The singers stood on risers in the middle of the mall.

"Up," Stewie said, when we stopped to watch. He kicked his legs. "Up." I started to leave, but Tanja didn't budge. She just stood there as if she were hypnotized or something.

"Tanja . . ." I began, and then stopped, realizing all at once what held her.

They were singing "O Tannenbaum." In German.

Tanja's lips moved to form the words, but no sound seemed to be coming out. She blinked, then swiped at her eyes.

So *this* was what homesick looked like.

The crowd shifted as some people in front left and some people in back moved forward. Tanja still didn't budge. A woman jostled me, and I bumped into the stroller. "Sorry, Stewie," I whispered, then reached down to pat his head.

He wasn't there.

"Stewie?" *We hadn't strapped him in!* I bent down and searched among the legs of the people around me.

No Stewie.

"Stewie!" I heard the scared sound in my voice. Tanja snapped out of her trance and looked at me. "I can't find Stewie!" I said.

"Ach du lieber Gott!"

We shoved through the crowd of people watching the carolers, whispering, "Stewie! Stewie!" We peered under the risers. We checked out the aisles of the shops nearby.

"Where can he be?" Tanja wailed.

Anywhere by now, I thought, but I didn't say it.

The mall was thick with people; the still crowd around the carolers was like an island surrounded by a moving ocean of shoppers. I was just about to climb onto a bench to see better when Tanja grabbed my arm.

"Look!" She pointed up and across the mall. "On those—how you say?—moving stairs!"

The escalator! Of course. There, near the top, bobbed a big red pompon.

I took off across the mall, dodging through the crowd like a football star going for a touchdown. The up escalator was jammed with people. By the time I reached the top, who knew where Stewie would be? But the down escalator had lots of room.

"Look out, here I come!" I yelled, hurtling up the down escalator. I pumped my legs hard against the never-ending downward movement of the steps, pushing myself to move up faster than they went down.

Look out! Someone coming down. I threw myself sideways to keep from slamming into the woman, then heard her furious scolding behind me. Now the escalator was blocked with angry, shouting people. "Coming through!" I said. One man refused to move; I hesitated, feeling myself going down, down, down, then dived through the tiny space between the man and his daughter. I scrambled upward and the crowd moved aside like the Red Sea parting, except now they were *really* mad. I slipped, banged my knee, grabbed for the rubber railing and, with a sudden burst of speed, sprawled out onto the floor beyond the escalator.

Where was Stewie?

I stood up and looked around. Through the crowd up ahead, I saw a bobbing red pompon. Stewie? But a woman was holding his hand. She was leading him away.

Was she *kidnapping* him?

I charged through the crowd, bumping into a teenager and knocking the packages from a fat lady's arms. At last I reached Stewie—it really was Stewie—and threw my arms around him from behind. But when I lifted him up, the woman wouldn't let go of his hand.

"What are you doing with my brother?" I said.

"Pardon?" She didn't look like a kidnapper. She was a

tall, plumpish woman with white hair and sharp blue eyes. "Is he your brother?"

"Yes. What are you doing with him?" I tried to pry Stewie away from the woman, but she wouldn't let go. Stewie began to cry. "Cany," he blubbered. "Mo cany."

"She gave you *candy?*" I said. "I knew it! They always do that!"

The woman's face reddened. "Now just a moment, young lady. How do I know he's your brother? He doesn't seem very glad to see you."

"He is too my brother. Let go!"

"I'll do nothing of the sort. Where's your mother?"

"My mother's not here, and if you don't let go I'll call the cops." I yanked hard and Stewie almost slipped out of the woman's grip; he cut loose with an ear-piercing wail.

"Security!" the woman called.

"Kidnapper!" I yelled.

All at once we were surrounded by a ring of grown-ups, all shouting to be heard above Stewie's screams and everyone else's shouting. ". . . Claims she's his sister," I heard one woman say, and. ". . . Mother not here."

"She's kidnapping my brother!" I bellowed.

I felt a hail of sharp pains on my thighs; Stewie was kicking me. Then I heard a familiar voice and turned to see Tanja making her way through the crowd. She pulled something out of a bag—the Polaroid with Santa, I saw—and showed it to the woman. Then she flipped through her wallet and let the woman look at some cards in little plastic sleeves.

107

The crowd slowly drifted away. The woman let go of Stewie's hand and smiled at Tanja. Tanja held out her arms for Stewie; I let go of him, then bent to rub the hurting places on my legs.

". . . so kind of you to be concerned?" Tanja was saying to the woman.

"Oh, I like to help. I worry whenever I see a child alone. I do so love children. . . ."—the woman looked hard at me—". . . *most* children." And then she was gone, lost among the crowd of Christmas shoppers hurrying home to dinner.

". . . And I could not believe it when you did run up those—how do you call them?"

"Escalator," I said.

"Ya, those escalator that were coming down and you were going up? And you did say, 'Look out! Here I come!'" Tanja doubled over in a spasm of giggles so violent I was afraid she might drive off the road.

"I didn't say *that*, did I?"

"Ya! Ya you did! And you did bump into all those people coming down. 'Coming through!' you did say. You should have seen the looks their faces had on."

I smiled. I guess it must have looked pretty funny. "Well, the other escalator was blocked, and I had to get to Stewie. I didn't know how else to do it."

"I could *never* have done that—not in my life," Tanja said. "If you weren't with me, that lady would have brought Stewie completely to the police station."

108

I shrugged, trying to look bored, but secretly I was pleased. "It was no big deal," I said.

"No big deal! Ya, it was very big deal. You do have that . . . spunk, Aurora MacKenzie. More than anyone else, I think."

"Even Helga?" I asked shyly.

"Ya," Tanja said. "More spunk than my spunky niece Helga."

BOARDING SCHOOL

Mom and Benjamin were not amused.

"How could the two of you *not notice* that Stewie was gone?" Benjamin asked at dinner when we told about Stewie's great escape.

Tanja's cheeks turned pink. "He did get out of his stroller and . . ." She shut her mouth and swallowed. "He does really walk fast," she finished lamely.

"That kid can *move*," I said. "All you have to do is look the other way for one second and—poof!—he's gone."

"I should think, that being the case, that you'd be doubly careful."

"Well, we were, except . . ." I turned to Mom for help. "You know how he is. It's impossible to keep him out of trouble all the time. Even *you* can't do it."

"That's true. Stewie does have a knack for trouble. But—" Mom looked at Tanja, then away again—"he ought to have been strapped in."

110

There was an awkward silence. I had the strangest feeling that something was going on I didn't know about. Everyone seemed to be concentrating on the pasta; the only sound was the scrape of forks on plates.

Then Mom started talking about the trip she and Benjamin were taking in a week, a weekend with friends in San Francisco. Benjamin asked if anyone had seen his golf shoes (Mom said they were in the garage) and Tanja asked if anyone had seen Stewie's red mittens (no one had).

So I said, "Did anybody see a purple notebook lying around here before dinner? I think I left it on the table, and now I can't find it."

Benjamin gave Mom one of his glances. "Have you looked in your room?" she asked.

"It wasn't *in* my room. I left it on the table."

"If you'd put your things away, Aurora, you wouldn't have these problems."

Why didn't she say that to Benjamin about his golf shoes? It wasn't fair. Still, something stirred uneasily in the pit of my stomach.

"But did you *see* it?" I asked.

"Uh oh. Is it seven-thirty already?" Benjamin wiped his mouth with his napkin and pushed his chair back. "I'll be late to my meeting if I don't get going."

Mom got up and walked him to the door. Stewie cried to be let down. Tanja unstrapped Stewie, put him on the floor, and began to clear the table.

"Can't anybody answer a simple question around here?"

I muttered. No one answered, naturally. I sighed, cleared my plate, and clumped upstairs to my room.

The notebook wasn't there either. I sorted through the piles of stuff on my desk and dresser, and rooted through the clothes on the floor.

Great. Just great.

I skipped back in my mind, trying to remember exactly what I'd written in my notebook. There was a page and a half about the van-denting incident. I had written everything about that. Otherwise, it was mostly bits and pieces. *Lets Stewie destroy property* and the business with the shoes in the toilet. *Endangers Stewie's life* and the falling-off-the-piano incident. *Boy crazy. Party animal.*

What would Mom think if she read that stuff?

I felt a funny pang as something else occurred to me.

What would *Tanja* think?

Then the phone rang, and it was Patsy. And what she had to tell me was so shocking that I forgot all about the notebook.

"Boarding school?" I asked. "Instead of Amsterdam?"

"That's what she told me," Patsy said.

"Why is Jessica going to boarding school?"

"She said it was for a 'higher quality education.' Whatever that means. She told me the boarding school costs a whole bunch, and it's so good she'll probably be a whole grade ahead of us when she comes back to our school."

"Will she *live* at the school? In *California?*"

"That's what boarding school means, Aurora."

"I know, but . . ." *Boarding school.* I remembered an old movie I once saw about a kid who went to boarding school. Rows of ugly iron beds. Dingy gray rooms with bars on the windows. Corn mush for dinner every night. "Does Jessica *want* to go to boarding school?"

"Well, she says she does. You know Jessica. She was bragging about how much it cost and how they have horses and a swimming pool and everything."

"In boarding school? They don't have that stuff."

"Yeah they do, nowadays. But, well, it looked like she'd been crying." There was a pause. "My mom says—promise you won't tell?"

"Promise."

"She says she thinks Jessica's parents are sending her to boarding school because she'd be too much of a handful in Amsterdam."

"What do you mean, 'handful?'"

"Well, you know how Jessica's always wising off to them, and how she hardly ever does what they say without arguing first?"

I swallowed. "Yeah?"

"Well, my mom says if Jessica keeps up this way, she'll be impossible when she gets to be a teenager. And so maybe her parents are trying to get her straightened out while they're gone."

"Wow." I'd never *heard* of being sent to boarding school before. Well, just in old movies. Never in real life.

I wasn't as much of a . . . handful . . . as Jessica, was I?
Boarding school. The thought of it gave me the creeps.

My purple notebook turned up a couple of days later in a pile of stuff on top of my desk. I was looking for some graph paper for a math assignment, and there it was. I could have missed it when I'd looked before; things disappeared and reappeared in my room all the time. But I clearly remembered leaving it on the kitchen table. I could picture it there. So how had it gotten on my desk?

Could Tanja have taken it? But she didn't act as if she'd found a secret notebook where I wrote bad stuff about her. She was acting really friendly, inviting me into her room, asking my advice on clothes, telling me about the pictures in her albums. And anyway, even if she had taken the notebook, why would she have given it back? Wouldn't she have destroyed the evidence?

Most likely it was Mom and Benjamin. Although it made me mad to think of them being that sneaky. But wouldn't they have *done* something? Maybe they wouldn't have sent Tanja back to Germany, but wouldn't she have gotten into some trouble, at least? But I didn't see any signs of trouble. Even with the van. One day Mom had taken it to the shop to get it fixed—that was all. Tanja hadn't even been grounded, or anything.

I didn't get it. I flipped through the notebook, remembering how excited I'd been about my plan. But now the things I'd written seemed . . . I don't know . . . mean. Or maybe not exactly mean, but . . . petty. That was the

114

word. Anyway, Tanja wasn't really all that bad. She really wasn't bad at all.

I shut the notebook and stuffed it into the bottom of my underwear drawer.

It was a dumb plan, anyway.

That night after I had gone to bed, I thought I heard crying in Tanja's bedroom. I lay there in the dark, wondering what to do. Just as I was about to get up and knock on Tanja's door, I heard footsteps.

"Tanja?" Mom's voice.

I heard the door open, then voices, then the door clicking shut. I got out of bed and lay down on the floor with my ear to the vent.

It was hard to hear through the whooshing of the furnace. Also, they were talking really softly. But then, for a second, Mom's voice came through clearly. ". . . like a dear, dear daughter to me," she said.

I couldn't make out what Tanja said back; it sounded sniffly and garbled. Then Mom's voice came again.

"Difficult . . . Aurora . . . easier with just a baby to care for."

My stomach curdled. I strained to make out the words in Tanja's rising voice, but couldn't, not quite. It sounded muffled, sort of, as though she were holding something over her mouth. I thought I heard Tanja say . . . "so much better . . . do really like her . . ." but I couldn't be sure.

Then Mom said something about ". . . Aurora . . . staying in California."

California. That was where the boarding school was!

I pressed against the vent until the metal cut into my ear. The voices were softer now. At last the whoosh of the furnace stopped and Mom's voice came again. ". . . best for everyone . . . not tell Aurora yet . . . find out soon enough . . . time to say good-bye."

I heard footsteps and the click of the door latch. Something was closing up inside me, cramping into a tight, hard ball.

They were sending me to boarding school.

I heard Tanja's door thud shut, heard the sound of Mom's feet on the stairs. I lay on the floor, my pulse pounding in my throat, trying to make myself believe what I'd heard. Things were clicking into place—things I'd seen and heard over the past couple of days but hadn't paid much attention to. The way Mom and Benjamin stopped talking once when I came into the room. The mysterious "meeting" Tanja and Mom had gone to that afternoon. Tanja's red eyes that night at dinner.

Once, I had heard Mom talking to Jessica's mother on the phone about boarding school. "It sounds like a positive move," she had said. "Best for everyone." I had thought she was just saying that to make Jessica's mother feel good. Now I knew better.

And Mom and Benjamin's trip next weekend. To *California.* They probably had to be there in person to sign me up for boarding school.

They were getting rid of me. I was too difficult for Tanja. She'd probably told on me, about the brownies and the slugs and everything. So Benjamin and Mom got to thinking—again—and they never even told me—again—and they were sending me away.

Tanja did seem to be sorry about it. But that was just too bad. If she were gone, Mom would have to stay home and there'd be no reason to send me away. Benjamin would see what a bad idea Tanja was in the first place.

I didn't feel good about what I was going to do, but I refused to be kicked out of my very own family.

Plan *D* was already starting to come to me.

It was a killer.

DIAL T FOR TROUBLE

*H*ello?"

Good. Patsy had answered the phone. "Ya, and is this Patsy Callahan which I am speaking to?" I asked.

"Yes, this is Patsy."

"Ya, and this is Elsa," I said, "the au pair girl from Stuttgart? And how are you today?"

"Uh, fine," Patsy said.

"And tchoost it is I vas vondering, vat is a nice girl like you doing to be friends with such brat like Aurora MacKenzie?"

There was a pause. Patsy said, "Who is this *really?*"

"Already I haf said it. I am Elsa. Only I vish to know vat you see in such—how do you say the vord?—rewolting scuzz like that Aurora?"

"Aurora, is that you?"

"No, tchoost it is me, Elsa, and I vould like only to know—"

118

"Aurora, cut it out! Cheez!"

Drat! "How'd you know it was me?" I said.

"*Revolting scuzz?* Give me a break, Aurora. I'm not totally stupid."

"Okay, but what else? You said, 'Who is this?' before I said 'revolting scuzz.'"

"I don't know. I just knew. Elsa wouldn't say stuff like that. She wouldn't call you a brat."

"Wanna bet?" I muttered. "Okay, but what about my accent? Wasn't it great?"

"I don't know. Not too bad, I guess," Patsy admitted. "But the more you talked, the less I believed you. Look, I've got to hang up now. My mom wants me to set the table and—"

"No, wait, Patsy! Don't hang up." She *couldn't* hang up. I was desperate. "I've got to tell you my plan."

"*Another* plan? Those plans of yours don't work, Aurora, in case you haven't noticed. My brother's still mad about the slugs. My parents made me apologize and clean the slime off the inside of the slug bowl to make up for it. Yuck!"

"I'm sorry, all right? You told me that fifty times already."

"Yeah, well, it's kind of hard to forget."

"But this is *different*," I said. "This will get rid of Tanja for sure. All you have to do is practice your German accent—I'll help—and then call Tanja Saturday night. I'll take care of everything else! I promise! Just tell Tanja you're Elsa and you ran out of gas on the way home from your

119

boyfriend's house on Mount Hood. Ask her to come get you."

"Aurora—"

I went on in a rush. "My parents will be in California this weekend! And Elsa's boyfriend's car is in the shop again—I heard Tanja say so. Don't you get it? And Tanja will *have* to rescue Elsa, so she'll leave Stewie and me alone. Then I'll call up our neighbor, see, and my parents will find out that Tanja left us all alone, and for sure they'll send her back to Germany."

"Aurora, that is the dumbest idea you've ever had. First off, she'd never believe I was Elsa—"

"I've got it all figured out. Trust me. You put a handkerchief over the phone. Then you get a radio and put it between stations where you can only hear static. So she thinks she's got a bad connection and she can barely hear—"

"I can't believe this, Aurora. You're telling me to lure Tanja away from you and Stewie in the middle of the night? Even if it did work—which it wouldn't—if my parents ever found out, I'd be cleaning slug bowls for the rest of my life."

"No one will find out, Patsy, I promise."

"That's what you said about the slugs."

"I know, but—"

"Aurora. This isn't fun anymore. Tanja could really get in trouble, and I . . . I feel kind of sorry for her. You might even get to like her, you know, if you'd give her a chance—"

120

"Oh, great. Just great. Now you sound like *Benjamin*." I swallowed against the tightness in my throat.

But Patsy was right. It wasn't any fun. I was trying to make it fun, and when I thought just about the details it was almost fun, almost like the old plans I used to do, before Tanja. But every time I thought about the *reason* for the plan, I got this sour feeling in my stomach, like when you drink a glass of chocolate milk and you expect it to taste good because it usually does, only now it doesn't because there's something really wrong with it.

It wasn't fun—but I had to do it. Anyway, Tanja had another family, in Germany. This was my *only* family. I wanted to be *here*.

"You don't even know, Patsy," I said. My voice came out a hoarse whisper. "You have no idea how bad it is." I slammed down the phone.

Who needed Patsy anyway? I was an expert on plans. I could do it all by myself.

"Hello? Chevron."

It was a man's voice. "Hello," I said, trying to make my voice low and grown-up sounding. "What time do you close at night?"

"Ten, Monday through Thursday. One, Fridays and Saturdays. Nine on Sundays."

"That one is . . . one in the morning?"

"Yep. Thanks for calling now. Bye."

"Wait!" Drat! Why did my voice have to squeak like

121

that? "Do you . . . I just wanted to know, like . . . do you have a phone booth there? Outside the gas station?"

"Sure do." Pause. "Listen, kid, are you in some kind of trouble?"

"No, I'm not in trouble." Shoot. How did he know I was a kid? "But . . . that phone booth is open? At night?"

"Yeah it is. Why—"

"And you're right on that road, that one that goes up Mount Hood?"

"Yeah, Highway Twenty-six. Why do you want to know? Is this some kind of quiz or what? Do I win a shopping spree at Toys "R" Us?"

Funny. Very funny. "No, I was just . . . just wondering. Bye."

I hung up, then cleared a place on my desk, opened my spy notebook and wrote, *Closes 1 A.M. Chevron station on road to Mt. Hood. Phone booth.*

Okay. Things were coming together. Mom and Benjamin had left for San Francisco on Thursday morning while I was in school. Tomorrow was Saturday, and tomorrow night was the night of Plan *D*.

Carefully, I reviewed my plan. I would set my alarm clock for 1:00 in the morning and put it under my pillow so it wouldn't wake Tanja. I'd get a handkerchief and my radio, tuned to receive only static. Then I'd call Tanja's private number.

Make it quick. Remember what Patsy said: The more I talked, the less Patsy believed me. After I hung up, I'd crawl back in bed and pretend to be asleep.

What if Tanja wanted to call Elsa's house and ask someone there to go get her?

She wouldn't. Elsa wasn't supposed to go up to her boyfriend's house at night alone. Tanja couldn't call Gudrun or Holly either because their families would find out. And she wouldn't call Elsa's boyfriend because his car was in the shop.

As soon as Tanja left, I would call Mrs. Sandberg next door to say I was afraid because Stewie and I were all alone. Maybe I'd say I heard noises.

Mom and Benjamin would find out Tanja had left us alone in the middle of the night. Elsa would say she never called. Mom and Benjamin would think Tanja was irresponsible and send her back to Germany.

The top of my head felt numb from juggling all the details of Plan D. But it was good. Not fun, but good. This plan was going to work.

It *had* to.

"Hello?"

Tanja's voice sounded sleepy. My palms were sweating; I wiped the one not holding the phone on my pajamas. I picked up an old T-shirt—I couldn't find a handkerchief—and wrapped it around the telephone mouthpiece. Then I hunched over the radio to make sure Tanja could hear the static.

"Hello?" Tanja said again. "Who is this?"

"It is Elsa?" I said, making sure not to squeak. "Oh, Tanja, please come help. I haf run out of gas in the wan, and I do need that you come to get me."

"What? Elsa? I can't hear you, there is such . . ." and Tanja said something in German.

German! I forgot that Tanja and Elsa would speak German. I let go of the T-shirt and left it dangling from the phone for a moment while I turned up the static on the radio. *Think. Think.* I'd just have to go on in English and hope that Tanja would do the same.

I repositioned the T-shirt and turned down the static a bit. "We do haf bad connection, and I cannot hear you? I haf run out of gas! I am at Chevron gas station, on Mount Hood on Route Twenty-six. Please, Henry's car has broke and so you must come get me!"

Tanja said something else in German; I heard Stewie's and my names. What did she say? Never mind; I would pretend I understood.

"Leaf them home," I said. "They will never know you haf gone. Tanja please! I do haf to go now. Do not tell *anyone* or I vill be in trouble! Tchoost come!"

I turned up the radio as high as it would go, held the phone near the static for a long moment, then hung up. I untangled the T-shirt from the phone and stashed it and the radio under my bed. I slid beneath the covers. Through the thumping of my heart, I strained to hear what Tanja was doing. I thought I heard her say something, and then it was silent.

Did she go back to bed? Maybe she didn't understand me because of the static. Maybe she guessed it was a trick.

124

But then I heard a rustling noise, then footsteps, then the sounds of drawers opening and closing.

It worked! She was getting dressed!

Footsteps. Quickly, I snuggled down into the covers and shut my eyes. I could hear my door opening.

"Aurora?"

I didn't move.

"Aurora!" Tanja shook me gently.

I moaned a little bit and slowly opened my eyes. "Hunh? What—?" I said.

"Aurora, I have to tell you something and I have to trust you not to tell anyone. Elsa is in trouble. She did call me from a gas station on Mount Hood where her car has run out of gas."

I rubbed my eyes and yawned. "Why doesn't she just buy some gas if she's at a gas station?"

"It is closed by now. We have to go to the all-night station in Gladstone and take her gas in a can.

We? I sat straight up. "*Who* has to?"

"We do. You and I and Stewie." Tanja touched my arm. "Elsa has done something . . . not very good. She has driven alone to her boyfriend's house, and she is not allowed to do this. Now it is very late. Elsa's family doesn't wait up for her, but if they—or Gudrun's family or Holly's family—do find out where she has been, Elsa will be in trouble. So we do have to go. And we cannot tell anyone of this."

"Why don't I baby-sit Stewie? Then you won't have to get him up and everything."

125

"No!" Tanja's voice was so firm, it startled me. "It is my job to take care for you two, and I cannot leave you alone in middle of the night. Get dressed now. I will go to get Stewie."

"But . . ." *This wasn't supposed to happen. Tanja was putting her own frills on my plan, and now it wasn't going to work.* "Really, I don't mind. I'm old enough to baby-sit by myself anyway. We'll be fine."

"No. This is my job, Aurora. I will not leave you and Stewie alone."

I started to argue, but something in Tanja's face stopped me. She looked . . . I don't know . . . fierce. Somehow I knew that no matter how much I argued or begged, she wouldn't change her mind.

"All right, I'm getting dressed," I said. I threw back my covers and slipped out of bed.

My thoughts zinged around in my head as I pulled on my clothes. Plan *D* was falling apart; it was spinning out of control. Plan *E*, Plan *E*, I needed a Plan *E*. Okay, what if I told Mom that Tanja pulled Stewie and me out of bed and dragged us halfway up Mount Hood in the middle of the night. That was pretty bad, wasn't it? Then when it turned out that Elsa wasn't there, it would look as if Tanja made up the phone call.

But why would she do that?

I don't know. Maybe she was meeting someone up there? A guy, maybe?

Then why would she take Stewie and me?

I don't know.

A sudden chill swept over me, and I stopped in the middle of tying my shoe. Why was I doing this? Why were we all going halfway up Mount Hood in the middle of the night to a phone booth when there was nobody there? Why didn't I just tell Tanja it was all a dumb joke, before it was too late?

Boarding school, that was why.

With a hard tug, I finished tying the bow. Plan *E* would work. I didn't know how yet, but I would *make* it work.

BLIZZARD

I hadn't planned on the snow.

It didn't start until after we'd left the all-night gas station where Tanja filled the gas can Benjamin always leaves in the garage. When we turned off the interstate and headed up toward the mountain, I first noticed the splotches on the windshield. Raindrops, I thought. But they didn't act like raindrops. They were thicker than raindrops, and stuck around longer, refusing to budge until the wiper slapped them down.

"I think it's snowing," I said.

Tanja nodded grimly and hunched over the wheel. She'd been awfully quiet for the past couple of days.

Maybe she felt guilty because I was being sent away and she got to stay.

Soon, fat wet snowflakes swarmed like moths in the headlights' beams.

128

"It's *really* snowing," I said.

Tanja didn't answer.

For a while the road stayed clear, like a fudge ribbon across powdered sugar hills. But a thin, white glaze began to creep across it. Once, the van slowed for a moment and made a high, whiny noise as if Tanja had revved the motor. But she hadn't. I'd been watching. I turned to check on Stewie. He was zonked out in his car seat with his mouth wide open.

It was a good thing Tanja's driving had gotten better. Not that it was all that great. But the lurchings and grindings of her first weeks at the wheel had finally smoothed out so that I hardly ever had to hang on to the grab bar anymore.

Still . . . I closed my fingers around the cool vinyl of the grab bar. I didn't like this snow. Once, in the snow, Mom had skidded into a mailbox. And she was a *good* driver.

"Do they have snow in Stuttgart?" I asked.

"Sometimes," Tanja said. "But I am not fond to drive in it."

Great.

We *must* be getting close by now. I strained to follow the shape of the road, which was now completely white. Tree boughs, weighed down by fat pillows of snow, crisscrossed overhead.

The whiny noise again. We were slipping, slipping on the snow. Then something caught and the engine calmed and we were on our way uphill.

I stretched out my fingers. I'd been gripping the grab bar so hard, my whole hand felt cramped. I wiped my damp palm on my jacket and reached for the bar again.

How did I get us into this mess?

Boarding school. Plan *D*.

But why did we have to go all the way to the Chevron station? Tanja would get in plenty of trouble just for risking our lives in a blizzard halfway up Mount Hood in the middle of the night. Maybe . . . "Maybe we ought to turn back," I said.

"We do need to find Elsa," Tanja said. I could tell by her voice there was no point in arguing.

"But this is getting . . . dangerous, Tanja."

"What are you saying? That we should go home and leave Elsa to freeze? That we should call the police? Then they would call her family, and she would be wearing my boots."

"Your . . . boots? What do you mean?"

"Oh, no matter." Tanja fell silent again.

I looked out past the snowflakes that whirled in the headlights' beams to the shadowy-white hills in the distance. We *must* be getting close. My eyes ached from straining. I couldn't remember when last I'd seen a car. The whole world seemed eerily hushed; all I could hear was the rumble of the van's motor. I hung on to the sound, waiting for it to change, to get thin and shrill and whiny as the tires lost their grip.

And what would happen when we got to the gas station

and Tanja saw that Elsa wasn't there? Would she turn back then?

I studied Tanja's face. Through the darkness I could make out the tightness of her mouth, the determined set of her jaw.

She wouldn't turn back. We'd drive around all night looking for Elsa. We'd get stuck in a snowdrift and no one would find us for days.

What if I told Tanja that Elsa wasn't there? That it had all been a joke?

I tried to imagine Tanja laughing at how I had tricked her, but the picture wouldn't come.

Forget it. If anyone found out what I'd done, I'd be in so much trouble they'd probably lock me up in boarding school and never let me out.

The whining sound. The van was slipping. It slipped, and slipped, and kept on slipping. I clutched the grab bar, waiting for the jolt I knew would come, waiting to slide into the ditch. But then the engine sound sank to a growl, and we weren't slipping anymore. Slowly, the van began to crawl uphill.

I let out my breath. My heart was thumping like crazy.

"Phew." Tanja pushed a strand of hair from her eyes, and I saw that her hand was shaking. "I did not know . . . how that would come out." She leaned forward to peer over the wheel. "But I think I do now see it," she said. "The gas station."

Staring hard through the snow-speckled dark, I found

the shape of the Chevron sign and then, at last, the squat gas station building itself.

It was deserted. Yellow light shone dimly through a window. Snow lay in a smooth carpet on the driveway, unbroken by footprints or tire tracks. The phone booth stood by the road, its door partway open. Snow drifted in a heap upon its floor.

Tanja eased the van into the driveway, then drove slowly past the building, searching, I knew, for Elsa's blue van.

It wasn't there, of course.

Tanja circled the gas pumps. "She did say Chevron station. I know I did hear that." Her voice sounded small and scared.

I was thinking fast. *Maybe*, I could say, *someone was driving on the highway. Maybe they saw Elsa and loaned her some gas. Maybe she's already home.*

Tanja cut the engine. Silence echoed in my ears. "Maybe . . ." I began. But the rest of the words stuck in my throat. I couldn't make them come.

"What?" Tanja asked.

I shrugged. "Nothing."

"I should look inside that window," Tanja said. "And in the back."

I felt my eyes drawn toward the building. It looked spooky. Sinister, even. Like on TV when the bad guy says to meet him alone someplace, and it's always spooky, and it's always a trap. "Do you think you'd better?" I asked.

"Yes. Please, the flashlight?"

132

"No, Tanja. Maybe you'd better not."

Tanja leaned across me and fumbled with the latch on the glove compartment, but her hands were shaking so hard, she couldn't make it work. I opened it for her and handed her the flashlight. "You stay here with Stewie," she said. "Lock the doors. Don't open them for anybody but me or Elsa, no matter what does happen." She smiled quickly and squeezed my knee. "Thank heavens you are my spunky girl," she said, then opened the door and stepped outside.

I watched the snowflakes' hushed dance in the flashlight beam as Tanja drew near to the darkened building. How could Tanja do that when she was so scared? Even I was scared, and I was the one who had spunk. So how could Tanja—the crybaby, the *spätzle* noodle—go out there all by herself?

Tanja disappeared around the side of the gas station; only a faint glow rimmed the edge of the building.

It was for Elsa. For Tanja's friend. Tanja was doing this to keep Elsa out of trouble.

The flashlight's glow faded and disappeared. The building was dark. *What's taking her so long?*

At last, light puddled onto the snow on the far side of the gas station, and I saw the dark shape of Tanja. She broke into a run, flinging wild flares of light across the snow. I unlocked the door and shoved it open.

"Is something out there? Why did you run?"

Tanja climbed in. "Elsa . . . is . . . not . . . here," she

133

said, gulping air. "And I . . . could not stand it . . . to stay out there anymore. I am such . . . how you say it . . . scaredy mouse?"

"Scaredy *cat*," I said. "And you're not."

"Yes, I—" Tanja choked on her words and seemed about to cry. She bowed her head, pressed her fist against her chin.

I watched Tanja's breath form puffs in the air, watched each new puff as it gobbled the last.

"Tanja?"

"Yes?"

"Can we go home now?"

Tanja heaved a shaky sigh. "No," she said, turning to me. "We must find Elsa. We will go next to her boyfriend's house, and if she is not there, then we will see what we will do."

"But she's n—"

"What?"

I stopped myself. "Nothing."

The engine roared to life. The van crept up the drive toward the highway.

Toward another dark building. Through more slippery snow. I studied Tanja's face, the pinched line of her mouth, the out-thrust set of her chin.

"She won't be there," I heard myself say.

"We do not know that, Aurora. She was here, calling from this gas station, and now she is—"

"No she wasn't. Elsa wasn't here. I'm the one who called."

134

CONFESSION

What?" Tanja asked softly. The van slowed, eased backward and drifted to a stop.

The snowflakes looked like Styrofoam. Like shredded Styrofoam cups that someone was shaking down from the sky.

"Aurora? It was you? It was you that called?"

I nodded.

"Why?" Tanja's voice was a whisper.

"I . . ." My throat closed up. No more words would come out. I shrugged.

"You were trying to . . . have me in trouble?"

I didn't answer.

"Were you? Is that what you were trying to do?"

I nodded.

"*Verdammt noch mal!*" Tanja's fist crashed down on the steering wheel.

Shocked, I stole a look at Tanja, then shrank from the hurt in her eyes.

"I did want to be your friend with you. I did think you *were* my friend because things have been lately going . . . going so well with ourselves. And now you do this?" Tanja let out a short, hard breath. "Why? Why do you do these things to me? Why do you hate me?"

"I don't—"

"No! I do want an answer. A *true* answer, for this one time. Tell me why!"

"I don't . . . I just . . ." Something was pushing up inside me and I couldn't hold it back. "I don't want to go to boarding school! I want to stay here!"

"What? Boarding school? What are you saying?"

"You know what I'm talking about! I heard you and Mom in your room. They're sending me to California!"

"Yes, but this has nothing to do with me. Your father—"

"They never listen to what *I* want to do. They just go around changing everything I like without even asking me. And now they're sending me away. They're . . . they're kicking me out! And it's all your fault because you told on me."

"No, it is your father—"

"It's Benjamin's fault, but it's your fault too! I heard you and Mom talking. They're sending me to boarding school because I'm too *difficult* for you. You can't *deal* with me. It would be *easier* with just Stewie. I bet you told them about the slugs and everything else. So now *you* get to stay here with *my* family, and I'm getting kicked out!"

136

"You think I did tell them. . . ." Tanja looked bewildered for a moment; but then she shook her head. "No, Aurora. You have it reversed the wrong way. *I* am the one getting—how you say it—kicked out. Because of *you*. Because your parents think I am not strong enough to cope with you. Because—"

"That's not true! I heard!"

"Well, you did hear it wrong, Aurora. Wrong. And you did write in that book—"

"What book? I don't write in books!"

"—that book with the lines in it and—how you say—the curly wire? How Stewie did fall off the piano. And the dent in the van. And I—"

"I didn't show that to anyone! Somebody must have—"

"—I was just going to tell of this, and so now your parents do think I am not responsible to care for you both or to drive the van or . . . or anything! And I am not supposed to tell you this, but I don't care anymore. I just don't care!"

Tanja put the van in gear and gunned the motor. The rear of the van slipped sickeningly in the snow, then the tires caught hold and the van roared up the drive, bounced, and skidded onto the highway. I clutched the grab bar, pressing myself back against my seat.

Tanja going away. Could it be true?

And she hadn't told on me—at least, that's what she said.

A whole bunch of feelings churned around inside me:

137

dread and anger and guilt all confusingly tangled together. But Tanja . . .

"Tanja, I didn't mean . . . I really don't hate—"

"Just don't talk to me, Aurora. I don't want to hear it. I don't care what you say anymore."

The trip down the mountain was awful.

Awful, because of the snow, which *wouldn't* stop coming, even when the road flattened out and connected with the interstate. My eyes burned from straining to see ahead; my whole arm ached from clutching the grab bar for so long.

Worse than awful, because of the poisonous silence in the air. It hurt my lungs, like breathing smog.

After what seemed like a week, the van pulled into our garage. I waited for Tanja to unlock the door, then went straight upstairs to bed.

But I couldn't go to sleep. Not for a very long time.

TOO LATE

I must have slept at last, because when I opened my eyes it was morning, with the sun slanting in pale stripes through the cracks in my blinds.

Lying in bed, I could hear Stewie babbling downstairs. There was a clank of dishes, a hiss of running water. I looked at my clock: 11:04. In my entire life, I'd never stayed in bed past ten.

Another voice: Tanja. All at once, the memory of last night came back in a sickening wave.

I couldn't go downstairs. Not yet. Not with Tanja there.

My stomach growled. I pushed aside my covers and rummaged through my top desk drawer for the economy-size bag of peanut M&M's Jessica had given me. It had cost me two Beach Boys posters and a hot-pink mechanical pencil. I was about to tear open the bag when I heard the garage door rumble open.

Mom and Benjamin. I ran to my window in time to see Benjamin's car drive through the melting snow and into the garage.

What should I do? Should I run downstairs and give my own version of what had happened last night, before Tanja had a chance to tell? Or should I wait and see what happened?

Tanja's voice. The front door opening. Stewie squealing "Mama!" and a swell of adult voices, Mom and Benjamin and Tanja. Then the other voices quieted, and Tanja's went on and on.

She was telling. I knew it.

I opened my door a crack and strained to hear, but I couldn't make out the words.

She must be telling. Why else would she be talking so long?

Footsteps on the stairs. I tiptoed back to my bed, slid beneath the covers, and pretended to be asleep. I heard the brush of my door across the carpet, felt a change in the air of the room.

"Aurora?"

Mom's voice.

The edge of the bed dipped, and I felt Mom's hand sweeping the hair from my face. I opened my eyes.

"Honey?" Mom said. "Tanja told me . . ."

My heart clutched. "I didn't know it was going to snow!" I said. "I wouldn't have done it if I did. And anyway I tried to get Tanja to come home after the van started slipping, but she just kept going up the mountain and so

140

I . . ." I trailed off. Mom was looking at me as if I had lost my mind.

"What's this?" she asked. "About the van slipping? And the mountain?"

"Nothing. I just—" So Tanja *hadn't* told.

"Aurora." I heard the warning in Mom's voice. I swallowed hard.

"Aurora, *tell me about the mountain.*"

I told.

I was tempted to make it sound as if it were a little bit Tanja's fault, except I kept remembering: Tanja didn't tell. So I didn't. I stuck pretty much to exactly what really happened until near the very end when—I couldn't help it—the story dropped away from me and my voice slipped up to a squeak. "I only did it because I wanted to stay with you. I don't want to go to boarding school. You're *not* going to make me, are you?"

A funny expression came over Mom's face, and I couldn't tell if she were going to laugh or cry, going to kiss me or spank me or strangle me. "Oh, Aurora," Mom said, shaking her head. "Aurora . . ."

She clasped me in a sudden, hard hug, then abruptly let me go.

"Don't you *ever* do anything like that again, do you understand me? *Ever.*"

I nodded.

"Do you realize what could have happened up there? What if you got in an accident? And there was nobody around for miles. . . ."

Mom's face changed, grew soft and kind of trembly. "This was all because you thought we were sending you away?"

I nodded again.

And then she was hugging me some more, but this time she didn't let go. I stiffened, thinking, I'm too old for this, but then my arms just sort of tightened and I pressed my face into Mom's neck and breathed in her perfume. "You're my specialest girl in the whole wide world," Mom whispered into my hair, and something inside me loosened, like a fist stretching open, its fingers numb from clenching for too long.

"Then I don't have to go?" I asked at last, pulling away.

"Honey, there's no question of boarding school," Mom said. "That never crossed our minds. But we were considering . . . your father wants to see you."

"Dad?"

"He's invited you to stay with them for Christmas. It'll be warm down in Malibu. You could go to Disneyland—"

"I don't *want* to go to Disneyland! Disneyland isn't Christmas. Christmas is telling stories and roasting marshmallows and opening everything Christmas Eve. The way we *used* to do, Mom. That was Christmas.

"But we can't tell stories anymore because Benjamin doesn't like to tell stories. We can't roast marshmallows anymore because they gum up our teeth. We can't even open our presents Christmas Eve because Benjamin likes to do it in the morning. And now you're sending me away!"

Mom was looking at me funny. Really *looking*. "Those things mean a lot to you, don't they?" she said.

"I told you they did. But you didn't listen. You never listen to me anymore. We used to plan things together, but now you and Benjamin get together and you do what *he* wants to do and what I want to do doesn't count. And you went and decided to send me to Dad's for Christmas, without even asking me. I bet that was Benjamin's idea too. I bet—"

"It isn't decided," Mom said. "Not for sure. I don't know how you found out about it and I'm not going to ask. But we were going to ask your opinion before we made a firm commitment."

"You mean I get to choose?"

Mom didn't answer right away. I could tell she was thinking, making up her mind.

"Yes," she said finally. "You can choose."

"Then I'm not going."

"All right. You don't have to. Not for Christmas."

I let out a huge sigh. I wasn't going away. Not to boarding school. Not for Christmas.

"But, honey," Mom said, "we'll have to work out another time for you to go." She brushed back my bangs, then sighed and leaned back against a pillow. "You know," she said, "I always felt guilty about the way we used to celebrate Christmas. We never even had a proper Christmas dinner. Remember the time we had macaroni and cheese?"

I nodded. "It was great."

Mom laughed and shook her head. "Oh, Aurora." She shook her head again. "I guess I always wanted to give you a real Christmas. Christmas with everything. Garlands and satin ribbons and a seven-foot noble fir. A lace and velvet Christmas dress. Wreaths all over the place. Ham and wild rice and baby glazed onions. But those things are expensive, and with just the two of us, it didn't make much sense. And then these past two years, when I *could* give you those things, you hated them."

"I told you that before you did them, but you didn't listen. You never listen anymore. I have to commit practically a capital crime to get you to pay attention."

"Okay. I'm paying attention now."

"I don't like it when you work. It's not fair Benjamin gets you all the time. And I want to have fun dinners, like we used to. And I want marshmallows on Christmas Eve, and brownies after school. And I want to make plans for us again like I used to, and not have you and Benjamin decide everything by yourselves. And—"

"Aurora, Aurora." Mom propped herself up on an elbow and looked at me. "We can't go back to the way things were. This is our life now. You didn't choose it, I know. But you have to accept it. You'll always be my specialest girl . . . but I love Benjamin and I love Stewie too. And . . . I love my job. It's not for Benjamin. It's for *me*."

She slid her arm behind my shoulders and gave me a squeeze. "But maybe we can work something out about Christmas. I miss those marshmallows too. And those other plans of yours. I'll talk to Benjamin—no, the two of us will talk to Benjamin. After Tanja leaves—"

Tanja.

"You can work something out for Tanja too, can't you? You can let her stay too?"

Mom sighed. "Well," she said. "Tanja's case is a little bit different. . . ."

Something flopped over in my stomach.

"What do you mean, different?"

"The two of you weren't getting along. We thought it best to look into other options—"

"There you go again, making plans behind my back! Why didn't you ask *me?* You should have asked me first!"

"I did talk to you, if you'll remember," Mom said.

I remembered. I remembered all the other things I had done to make Tanja go away. The slugs. Calling Mrs. Stephanus. The spy notebook.

"Also, we had reason to believe that . . . ah . . . Tanja was lax in watching Stewie and . . . ah, the dent in the van, for instance . . ."

"You got that from my notebook! I never said you could read it, and—"

"Then why did you write those things down?"

Mom's look cut right through me. I couldn't answer.

"We were concerned about your welfare, Aurora. We did what we thought best for you." Mom sighed. "Maybe I should have seen . . . I don't know." She shook her head. "Mrs. Stephanus said to wait, that you'd have a change of heart, that things would work themselves out. I should have

145

listened to her, but . . . what's done is done. The new au pair is flying down from Seattle tonight, but she won't be staying here until after Tanja leaves. She . . ."

"*New au pair!*" There was an aching in my chest. "What about Tanja! What's going to happen to her?"

"Nothing bad, Aurora. She's just—"

"She's not going back to Germany, is she?"

"No, but—"

"Then let her stay. I *like* her, Mom! I want her here with us!"

"You can't have her, Aurora," Mom said gently. "It's too late."

PLAN G —
FOR GOOD-BYE

Too late.

Those words have such an awful sound to them. Like the last bell before school starts, when you're halfway down the hall and you've got two tardies already and the third one means you have to go to the principal's office.

Ring ring: too late.

Too late to take back all the mean things I did to Tanja and fix it so she can stay. Too late to make it up to her—too late to *face* her ever again.

I tried to get Mom to change her mind. For half an hour I tried. But after she explained it all to me—how many people are involved, how many plans have been made, how all the plans fit all together—then I had to admit that it really was too late.

Too late—and all my fault.

And I can't leave my room because I might run into

147

Tanja, but I can't stand it in here all alone with my thoughts going off like popcorn in my head and driving me crazy.

I need to talk to Patsy. Where is she?

I dial for the fourteenth time.

Ring.

Ring.

Ring.

"Hello?"

"Patsy, where've you been? I've been trying to reach you for ages!"

"Who is this? Godzilla? The Creature from the Black Lagoon?"

"Would you cut it out, Patsy, you know it's me. Listen, you have to come over right now."

"How come?"

"I can't come out of my room. I'm staying in here for three whole days and I hardly have any food left."

"Uh oh. Aurora. You didn't do that weird plan of yours, did you? Are you grounded forever?"

"Sort of and not exactly. I'll explain the whole thing when you come over. Are you busy now or something?"

"Well, no, but—"

"Good. See you in a minute."

I start to hang up.

"Oh, wait . . . Patsy?"

"Yeah?"

"Bring food."

* * *

Patsy smuggles up Twinkies and corn nuts and barbecue potato chips. I think I must be sick. They don't even taste good. I flop down on my bed and tell her everything that's happened.

"She's really leaving?" Patsy says when I'm through telling her. "You did it, Aurora. You won."

I shrug.

"What's wrong? You should be excited. This is what you wanted all along."

"I did, but . . . I don't know."

"Oh, I get it." Patsy grabs a handful of potato chips and leans back against the pillows on my bed. "You changed your mind."

I sigh. "I guess maybe she wasn't as bad as I thought."

Patsy crunches thoughtfully.

"I kind of . . . *like* her, actually."

Patsy raises her eyebrows.

"Oh, Patsy, don't you see? It's all my fault she has to go. And I bet she'll hate me forever, and I don't blame her if she does. And my mom says I have to say good-bye to her before she goes, but if I do she'll probably act nice on the outside while she's hating me on the inside and I really couldn't take that, Patsy. I couldn't . . . *look* at her while she was doing that. Do you see what I'm saying? Have you ever felt that way?"

"I don't know," Patsy says slowly, "I think maybe a little. But . . . can't you do something about it? Think of another plan! You're the expert on plans, Aurora. What about Plan G for *Get Tanja Back?*"

"I'm only up to *F*."

"Okay, so Plan *F* for *Find a Way to Keep Tanja Here*. Who cares what you call it? Come on, Aurora! *Think* of something!"

"I can't, Patsy. It's too late. Tanja's going to San Diego to be an au pair for a family there, and another au pair named Carol is coming here from where she was an au pair in Seattle. She's staying with Mrs. Stephanus until Tanja leaves on Wednesday."

"Why can't you just tell this Carol to stay in Seattle?"

"Because there's *another* au pair on the way from somewhere else—I don't know where—to take Carol's job. Don't you get it? They've got this whole thing worked out and every part of it is hooked up to every other part and some of the parts are already happening. It's all set. There's nothing I can do."

"Oh." Patsy looks disappointed.

"Those plans were dumb, anyway," I say. "They never did any good."

"Well, one of them sure did something."

"Gee, thanks for reminding me."

"Sorry."

I pick at the little chenille bumps on my bedspread. There's an achy feeling pressing against my heart. Patsy just sits there a minute and then she starts talking about a big party Jessica's parents are throwing for her.

"They're having two different Elvis impersonators and a guy who makes balloon animals. And maybe a real live band."

Why? I thought Jessica's birthday was in March."

"This is a good-bye party, Aurora. Because of boarding school. And she's inviting practically the whole world. My mom says it's so she'll get more presents. . . ."

I stare at Patsy. A *good-bye party*.

". . . won't believe the cake they're going to get her," Patsy is saying. "It'll cover a whole table, and on top it's going to say . . ."

Good-bye party.

That's it. That's what I'll do. There's no way I can get Tanja to stay—it's too late for that now—Mom made that absolutely clear. But maybe I can make her not hate me. Maybe it's not too late to *face* her again.

I suck in a deep breath. Yeah, I'll skip Plan *F* and go straight to *G*.

Plan *G*—for Good-bye.

"Aurora?" Patsy says. "Did you hear me? About the cake?"

"Forget the cake," I say. "I've got a plan."

The trouble with some plans is you can't just decide what to do and then do it. You have to make other people believe in them first. Especially mothers.

"A good-bye party?" mine says later, when Tanja's gone to the store and I can go downstairs. "That almost sounds as if you're happy to see Tanja go. As if you're celebrating."

"No, it's not like that at all," I say.

"Couldn't we just call it a Christmas party, since it'll happen a week before Christmas?"

"No, Mom. This is for *Tanja*. It's . . . a plan to make her feel good. Not a mean kind of plan. It's to make up for all the other stuff—you know—the stuff that I did. . . ." So I can *face* her again, I'm thinking.

Another thing about mothers is they want to make sure you're not inviting too many people, but then they give you a whole list of people you're not allowed to leave out.

"You'd invite the other au pairs, wouldn't you?" mine says. "And Carol, the new au pair—we couldn't forget her."

"But she'll get all the glory, instead of Tanja," I say.

"Carol won't steal Tanja's thunder. It'll be a good chance for her to get to know us, that's all."

Also, mothers are *always* worried about money.

"*How* many Polaroids did you say you want to take?" mine asks. "A *hundred?*"

"It's for this thing I have planned," I say. "It's important."

"Do you know how much that'll cost? It's a small fortune in film. I know *you* don't have that kind of money, and I—"

"I have a little birthday money left—"

"About two dollars, if I remember correctly—"

"Four dollars and sixty-seven cents. And I could borrow the rest—"

"I'll pay for the film," Benjamin says.

I look up, amazed. I didn't even know he was listening.

"It's a worthwhile project, Shelley," he says. "Aurora's organizing this whole thing on her own, and I think she

152

deserves a lot of credit. If she finagles the rest of this shindig, I'll cover the film."

Sometimes, stepfathers can surprise you.

The really hard part is avoiding Tanja for three days. I spend most of my out-of-school time at Patsy's and Jessica's, and the rest of it in my room. Patsy's mom takes us to the store and we buy crepe-paper streamers. At Jessica's we print up a WE'LL MISS YOU, TANJA banner on her computer.

We can't send out invitations in the mail because there's not enough time, so we have to call everybody. Nobody else wants to call the au pairs, so I volunteer.

"*You're* going to call them?" Patsy asks.

"Sure," I say. "Well, Gudrun at least. She can call the others."

"Do you think she'll believe you?"

"Don't be dumb," I say. "Of course she will."

But . . .

"This is one of your tricks, I do know it," Gudrun says when I call.

"No! It's not a tr—"

"I have had enough of you with your tricks and your lies, Aurora. Good-bye."

I shrug at Patsy, the dial tone buzzing in my ear. "Well," I say, "I tried."

It takes four more phone calls—one from me to Mom, the next from Mom to Gudrun, a third from Mom back to me, and the last from me to Gudrun again—before I can invite the au pairs.

"And they're taking care of all the food," I tell Patsy. "Holly's going to get Tanja out of the house, and Gudrun and Elsa will come over and cook a big German meal. Holly'll get Tanja home around six and everyone will be here already and then—"

"Surprise!" Patsy says.

"Right."

"Do you think she'll really be surprised?"

"If nobody tells. They'd *better* not."

Now Patsy looks uncertain. "And all the food's going to be . . . *German?*"

I nod.

"What's German food like?"

"Dis*gus*ting," I say cheerfully.

SO YOU
WON'T FORGET

Tanja *is* surprised.

I can tell by the look on her face when the front door opens and everyone yells, "Surprise!" It's the same wild-animal-in-the-headlights look she had at the airport that first day when I jumped out in the wolf man mask.

Then Tanja starts to cry (of course) and everyone moves in to comfort her (of course) and I start taking pictures.

Click! I get Tanja in a hug-huddle with Elsa and Holly and Gudrun. *Click!* I get Mom handing Tanja a dish towel to wipe the tears and mascara off her face. I get Benjamin sneaking a taste of frosting, Mrs. Stephanus checking a pan in the oven, and Stewie smearing dip into his hair.

Every time a photo pops out of the camera, I hand it to Patsy or Jessica, who runs upstairs to put it on my desk. When I finish the first package of film, I go up to my room to reload.

155

"Jessica and I could start putting pictures in the album," Patsy says. "Then you won't have to do it all at once."

"Thanks! That would be great. Only make sure you guys don't goof it up. I don't want Mrs. Stephanus's pictures labeled 'Stewie' or anything like that."

Click! I get Jessica sticking out her tongue.

The next time I reload, I find Mrs. Stephanus in my room, paging through the album. "This is for Tanja?" she asks. "From you?"

I nod. "But please don't tell her. Not yet."

"It's wonderful, Aurora. But . . . wouldn't it be nice if you had one of Carol? That would sort of round out the album, don't you think?"

Mom introduced me to Carol, the new au pair, before Tanja got here. "Carol was captain of her soccer team in New Zealand," Mom said. "She was practically a star."

I wasn't impressed. Carol has short, dark hair. She isn't as pretty as Tanja. She has an accent, but it isn't like Tanja's. Carol makes the words sound big and round, and her mouth takes a long time getting around them.

I like Tanja's accent better. I have no intention of putting Carol in the album.

I mumble something and race downstairs.

Click! I get Tanja and the rest of the Mafia lip-synching to a Beach Boys tape. *Click!* I get Mom and Benjamin doing the *cha-cha-cha*. I get Mrs. Stephanus dancing with Stewie's feet on her feet, Elsa limboing beneath a broomstick, and Stewie drumming the table with a bratwurst.

156

"How many of those are you going to take?" Benjamin asks. "You're driving me to the poorhouse."

Click! I get Benjamin turning his pockets inside out to show how poor he is.

I sit down for a minute near where Mom and Mrs. Stephanus are going through a big cardboard box full of old photographs.

"Here's Stewie at six months, one day at the zoo," Mom is saying. "He had four teeth already, do you believe it?"

She hands the picture to Mrs. Stephanus, then turns to me. "We were just looking at a cute one of you. You were about two and a half, and . . . wait a minute, I'll find it."

She digs through the box and pulls out a picture of a dark-haired baby girl sitting on the shoulders of a dark-haired man. My dad. "You used to grab his hair and steer him," Mom says. "I'm surprised he has any left."

The baby girl was smiling like crazy, bouncing on her father's shoulders. That was *me*, I tell myself. When we were living with my dad.

". . . embarrassed I've never put them into any kind of order," Mom is saying to Mrs. Stephanus. "Just stuffed them into a box."

I lean over and riffle through the pictures. There's one of Stewie when he was just born. His eyes look all squinty, and his nose is smushed to one side. There's one of me when I was six and had a hole where I should have had teeth. There's Mom and Benjamin at their wedding, and Mom and me on my first day of kindergarten, and Dad and me the last time I went to see him, three summers ago. He's holding one of my hands and one of my feet and he's swinging me into a swimming pool. I'm screaming and laughing like crazy.

The pictures are mixed in together as if all the changes —all the people coming into and going out of my life—were as natural as losing my front teeth, or growing out of last year's bathing suit.

I've been through a lot of changes, I guess.

But I don't have to like them.

But I always survive.

"Everybody come and get it!" Gudrun dings a spoon against a glass in the dining room. The table is heaped with food.

I take a giant slice of Black Forest cake and tiny spoonfuls of everything else. Then I sit down to eat with Patsy and Jessica on the floor by the living room window. Everyone's eating in here—on couches, on chairs brought in from the dining room, and on the floor. It was my idea. I just couldn't see us jammed all stiff and formal around the dining room table.

"Psst! What's this?" Patsy whispers, poking at something on her plate.

"Sauerbraten," I say. "Don't eat it."

"I love sauerbraten," Jessica says. She takes another bite. "Um. Yummy."

I make a gagging face, but carefully, so none of the au pairs can see.

158

The *käse spätzle* isn't bad, though, I have to admit. Kind of like macaroni and cheese. And the potato pancakes are actually pretty good. Not as good as french fries. But really okay. And the Black Forest cake is fantastic. I knew it would be. Germans are good at dessert.

Pretty soon everyone starts taking dishes into the kitchen. Benjamin puts a chair in the middle of the living room floor and motions for Tanja to sit in it. He makes a little speech about Tanja, and she starts crying again. Mom gives her a box of Kleenex with a red bow on top. Elsa and Gudrun and Holly bring in the presents from the den.

I kneel on the floor where I have a good view and take pictures of Tanja as she opens each present.

Click! I get the fancy nightgown from Gudrun. I get the bikini from Elsa, the Walkman radio from Holly, and the bath brushes from Mrs. Stephanus. I get the sweater from Mom and Benjamin and the Snoopy sweatshirt from Stewie. I get the Beach Boys tape from Patsy and Jessica.

Then I tear upstairs with the last of the Polaroids to put them in the album. I fumble with the stick-on labels and write as fast and as neatly as I can. *Nightgown—Gudrun. Bikini—Elsa.*

"Speed it up, slowpoke!" Jessica hisses from the doorway.

"I'm *hurrying!*" I write faster.

"Everybody's waiting!" Patsy says.

"Stop bugging me! Go down and tell them I'll be right there!"

Snoopy sweatshirt—Stewie. Beach Boys tape—Patsy and Jessica, I write. I put down my pen and close the album.

There.

All at once I feel shy, and a little bit scared. This is it. I can't put it off anymore.

Slowly, I walk down the hall. I pause at the top of the stairs.

"Aurora! Hurry up!" Jessica yells from the living room.

I start down the stairs. Benjamin is talking, saying something about ". . . be here in a moment. But in a way, this party is a gift from her. It was all her idea."

"*Aurora's* idea?" Tanja sounds surprised. I take a deep breath, then step into the living room.

"Aurora?" Tanja turns to look at me. "This party . . . was your idea?"

Everyone is looking at me now. I shrug. "Well, lots of people helped."

"Don't be so modest, Aurora," Benjamin says. "She organized the whole thing. Spent hours on it, working out the details. I was very impressed. She's quite a planner, this gal of ours."

"I do know this already," Tanja says, and there's a quiver at the edges of her mouth.

The grin spreads across my face all by itself; I don't do it on purpose. Something stings behind my eyes. Tanja isn't mad anymore. She definitely isn't mad. "Here," I say, and thrust the album into Tanja's hands.

"What is this? A photo album?" Tanja opens the album,

160

looks, slowly turns a page. "And these . . . are of tonight? These are pictures of tonight!" She turns to me, and the strangest look crosses her face. "How did you do this? Put them all in here together so quickly?"

"Patsy and Jessica helped," I say.

"Yeah, we did all the hard parts," Jessica puts in.

"But these photographs . . . are all for me? You did take them all for me?"

I nod. "So you . . ." My voice comes out hoarse, and my lips go all trembly and *won't* be still. ". . . won't forget us," I force out in a whisper.

Tanja sets down the album and smothers me in a hug. I gasp a quick, chokey breath, pressing my cheek against Tanja's sweater. "I'm sorry," I whisper. "I'm really, really sorry."

I feel Tanja's chest move in a sigh. "Well," she says at last, "you did have your own troubles, I think."

She pulls away, seems to study my face. She brushes something wet from my cheek. Then, "I will never forget you," Tanja says, soft and fierce. "Never."

Around us, I hear people moving. I hear Benjamin talking, something about "group photo" and "wide angle lens." I swallow, smile at Tanja, dab at my eyes.

Tanja takes my hand and leads me into the family room, where everyone is standing around waiting to get their pictures taken. Benjamin has set up a tripod and is fiddling with his camera.

". . . idiotic camera," he's saying. ". . . never *can* make it work."

Then Carol is standing beside him. "Let me take the picture," she says. "Then you can be in it and you won't need the timer."

"No, no. I've almost got it," Benjamin says.

"There's no reason for me to be in the picture, and anyway there isn't any room," Carol says.

All of a sudden I feel sorry for Carol, standing there with her stiff, too-smiley smile.

I slip my hand from Tanja's, grab Carol's hand and pull her in beside me. "There's plenty of room," I say.

"Yikes! The timer! It's going off!" The camera's whirring; Benjamin leaps in a mad rush to join us.

Click!

FAMILY ALBUM

It's a good picture, I think. Well, pretty good, anyway. There are some strange things about it, but those are the things I like best. Like the way Benjamin doesn't quite make it all the way into the picture. He has this funny, strained expression on his face, and his bald spot is bright pink, and half of his body is missing. Elsa is giving Tanja cooties, and Gudrun is giving *her* cooties, and I have two sets of cooties, from Patsy and Jessica.

Funny how I had no idea about those cooties.

The only bad thing about the picture is what happens at first, right when I pick it up and my eyes come to Tanja. There's this strange, sharp pang I feel then, in the middle of my chest.

But the pang isn't the picture's fault. It isn't Tanja's fault, either. I know whose fault it is—which is why the pang comes.

So I do what I always do when that happens: I bring the

163

picture closer—real close—and I look hard at Tanja's face. She's grinning. She's facing straight forward, but her eyes are turned toward me.

Then I take a deep breath, and the pang slowly fades.

My favorite part, I think, is the look on Carol's face. She's staring at me with her mouth wide open and her eyebrows arched almost to her scalp.

That's when I grabbed her and pulled her into the picture. I guess she was kind of surprised.

But then, Tanja was surprised too, the first time she met me. I guess I'm hard on au pairs, surprise-wise.

I sigh, and then slip the photograph under the clear plastic sheet that holds it in the album. It's taken me nearly six months to sort through the pictures in Mom's cardboard box and put them all in albums. There were pictures from way back when my grandmother was a child: unsmiling, black-and-white people who always wore hats.

I've filled eleven albums already, and I still have this whole big stack of photos left. Slowly, I flip through them. Here's Carol teaching me how to jump rope double Dutch. Here's Stewie sitting like a king on his new potty chair. Here's Jessica, home on vacation from boarding school, which truly *does* have horses and a swimming pool.

And here's Christmas. I still can't believe Benjamin ate five marshmallows, but I've got the picture to prove it right here.

At last, I come to the pictures I got in the mail last week.

They're of Tanja. Tanja holding the baby she's au pairing. Tanja hugging Mickey Mouse at Disneyland.

164

Tanja roller-skating on a sidewalk at the beach. Wearing a bathing suit. In *March*.

In the letter she sent, Tanja said she's coming to Oregon next October. She met an au pair in California who'll be through with her job at the end of September, same as Tanja. The au pairs get a month at the end of their terms just to travel around the United States. So Tanja is coming back here.

Patsy was really excited when she found out. "What are we going to do when she gets here?" she asked.

"Do?" I didn't get it.

"Yeah, *do*. I mean, we should have a plan. Like, she's coming in October, right? So we could get a whole bunch of us together and dress in spooky costumes. And when Tanja knocks at the door we could all jump out and yell *surprise*."

"We already did that, remember?"

"Not in costumes. That would *really* surprise her."

"I don't know, Patsy," I said. "Maybe Tanja's had enough surprises. Anyway, she's getting kind of old. She might have a heart attack or something."

"Nobody has heart attacks when they're nineteen."

"She's *twenty* now, remember?"

"Well, twenty either. I'm just saying, I think we should do something. A big sign, maybe, or . . ."

"Like a billboard?" I said.

"Yeah, like that. Or maybe one of those airplanes that pulls signs through the air behind it," Patsy said. " 'Welcome, Tanja!' Can't you just see it?"

"What about a skywriter? We could hire a skywriter!"

"Or a hot air balloon! I've always wanted to go up in one of those."

"That's great, Patsy! We could float right past the window of Tanja's plane! And everybody would look out and see the 'Welcome, Tanja' sign we were holding, and everybody would know it was for her. She'd freak out."

"I don't think they let you do that," Patsy said.

"Why not? I bet they would."

"Well . . . I don't know. Anyway, I have a feeling all this stuff costs a whole bunch. We'll probably have to think of something cheaper. But still . . . we have to do *something*."

Now I bend over the roller-skating photo and study Tanja. She *is* in pretty good shape. She probably won't keel over, no matter what we do. She might even enjoy it, once she gets over the shock.

Yeah, Patsy was right. We have to do *something*. Something nice, but outrageous.

Like what?

Well, there's still plenty of time. We'll write down all the ideas we can think of, then pick the best one later.

I dig through my underwear drawer until I come up with my old purple notebook. I cross out "Research," and flip through the pages until I come to a blank one.

Plan H, I write. *For Hello.*